Jessie and Ki were in deeply concentrated thought...

"It's too much of a mystery, and it makes my bones itch," Ki murmured in accompaniment to the hoof-beats of their jogging horses. "I can't help wondering just what this railroader Yates has up his sleeve that he couldn't tell you in his telegram."

"What beats me, Ki, is that Yates wired for help at all," Jessie answered. "He's never needed anyone's help before that I know of—he's reputedly bragged he could always take care of himself and his business."

They rode on slowly, side by side. As they approached the mouth of the little pass, a metal hornet buzzed between them, almost brushing against Jessie's shoulder. From downwind came the crack of a rifle...

WESLEY ELLIS

LONE STAR

AND THE MOON TRAIL FEUD

A JOVE BOOK

LONE STAR AND THE MOON TRAIL FEUD

A Jove Book/published by arrangement with
the author

PRINTING HISTORY
Jove edition/April 1985

ISBN: 0-515-08174-4

Chapter 1

As the tough pair of roan geldings loped along the rutted ore-wagon trail, their weary riders sagged in their saddles as if half asleep.

One of the riders was a woman. Tall, in her twenties, her body taut-breasted, lithe-hipped, and leggy, Jessica Starbuck had a sensuous way of moving—even when wearily astride a livery stable's ill-fitting saddle. She was clad in a snug-fitting blue cotton shirt, well-worn jeans and matching denim jacket, a broad brown leather belt, and riding boots. A summer's afternoon sun gleamed off stray wisps of her coppery blond hair, which she wore softly coiled beneath her flat-crowned hat. The sultry warmth extended to her tanned face, with its high cheekbones and wide, audacious green eyes. And yet, at the moment, her features couldn't help mirroring the exhausting effects of her long trip from the Circle Star Ranch in Texas to here, southeast of Seattle in the Washington Territory.

1

Jessie was making one of her rare trips to the Pacific Northwest, yet there was no particular need for her to keep alert in search of landmarks. She had a fair picture of the terrain in her mind from previous excursions, and from studying her extensive collection of maps before starting out weeks before.

From Seattle, on Puget Sound, a wide, rolling valley extends to the Cascade Range, the "backbone" of the territory. Rising some eight thousand feet above sea level, the Cascades comprise a broad mass of snow-clad peaks surrounded by virgin evergreen forests, the mountains very irregular and nearly inaccessible, being cut by intricate valleys and bulwarked with high ridges and glacier-carrying alpine meadows, lakes, cascades, and streams.

Within this range, especially along its rugged foothill terrain, was a rich abundance of fish and fur-bearing animals, as well as seemingly endless resources of fir, cedar, spruce, and select hardwoods. Yet, indirectly, it was the great mineral assets that had prompted Jessie to travel to this region. Not the usual gold, silver, or other metallic ores—of which there were relatively little—but coal.

Exploitation of coal had begun back in 1853, with the chief fields more to the north of where Jessie and her companion now rode. However, among the small yet potentially priceless holdings she'd inherited upon the death of the father, Alex Starbuck, were the Snowshoe Mines, which provided a low-grade bituminous variety. These mines were the only source of coking coal along the entire Pacific Coast. Somehow, in some way as yet undetermined, her Snowshoe operation was in trouble. And Jessie was on her way to find out how and why, and to do something about it.

So too was her riding companion, Ki. Like Jessie, Ki was tired; nevertheless he rode upright in his saddle, a man in his early thirties whose lean, sinewy body was graced with energy and agility. Born in Japan to an American sea

2

captain and his Nipponese wife, Ki had inherited his father's respectable height and natural endurance; from his mother he'd been blessed with his lustrous black hair and Oriental eyelids; while from both had come the handsome bronze tone of his complexion, denoting his mixed parentage.

Orphaned at an early age, Ki had learned how to survive in a hostile world as a half-breed outcast. Eventually he'd apprenticed himself to one of Japan's last master samurai, the aged Hirata, who had instructed Ki in the philosophies of the martial arts, and trained him in all forms of armed and unarmed combat. After Hirata's death, Ki had migrated to San Francisco, where he was hired by Alex Starbuck, the wealthy international business magnate. When, years later, Alex Starbuck was murdered, Ki became the confidant and protector of Starbuck's only child, Jessica, whom by then Ki had known for so long that he was like an older brother to her.

Those who were acquainted with Ki knew him to be calm yet alert by temperament, and utterly devoted to Jessie Starbuck and her far-flung interests. And, as one preferring to stay out of the limelight, he wore common range garb— faded jeans, a loose-fitting, collarless shirt, a worn black leather vest, and a battered flat-crowned Stetson. Of course, he did wear a pair of rope-soled cloth slippers, which, in this land of mining and lumberjack's boots, looked a bit unusual. So did his lack of a gunbelt, or any other sign of a firearm. Yet he was far from being unarmed—for in his vest were secreted short daggers and other small throwing weapons, including a supply of *shuriken*—little, razor-sharp, star-shaped steel disks.

These were not the only weapons the two riders carried. A custom-made Colt revolver was holstered on Jessie's right thigh, and a two-shot derringer was cunningly stashed behind her big brass belt buckle.

Their hands never strayed far from their respective weap-

3

ons, even though they had no specific reason to suspect they might be in danger. Moreover, they may have seemed half-asleep as they rode along, but in fact, now that they were nearing their destination, they were in deeply concentrated thought.

"It's a puzzle," Ki murmured in accompaniment to the hoofbeats of their jogging horses. "Too much of a mystery, and it makes my bones itch. I can't help wondering just what this railroader, this E. E. Yates, has up his sleeve that he couldn't tell you in his telegram."

Ki was recalling the terse note that Jessie had shown him when she'd called him into her ranch office and told him they were leaving on another mission.

"Ordinarily, when somebody asks for your help," Ki continued, "he's not shy about speaking right out, telling you what's bothering him, and calling for Starbuck to get busy—and just how, as well. But Mr. Yates was very vague."

"Vague!" Jessie smiled tightly and quoted the message: "'To salvage Snowshoe and situation, your presence required immediately.' Why, vague's hardly the word for it. What beats me, Ki, is that Yates wired for our help at all. He's never done it before, that I know of—he's reputedly bragged he could always take care of himself and his business, and didn't need anyone's help. And from all I've heard, he has, too—before."

"But now, I suppose," Ki said with his characteristic dry grin, "somebody has begun to play around in his preserve, somebody he can't lay his finger on, so he thinks he might as well finesse Starbuck into wading in on his side."

Jessie nodded. "Well, we've got investments to protect, both in Snowshoe and with him. I can't blame him for turning to us if there's a crisis looming he can't handle alone, or shouldn't handle personally, because it's not his concern."

4

"Such as Snowshoe Mines," Ki stated.

"Such as Snowshoe Mines," Jessie echoed in confirmation. "Yates doesn't own that company; Starbuck does. And this particular Starbuck was already aware that the mines weren't doing as well as expected. I just hadn't thought the problem—whatever it was—was as serious as Yates's telegram implied."

True enough. For a short while now, Jessie had known that Snowshoe's production was faltering, but had chalked it up to the fact that the company manager, Zachariah Baldwin, had died, thereby causing a disruption in the orderly flow of things. Baldwin's son, Ted, had been appointed to replace him on a trial basis; the young man had enough experience and engineering education to justify the promotion, but evidently he wasn't working out as well as hoped. That is, if subsequent production figures and Yates's between-the-lines message were to be believed.

Jessie had faith in both. Her accountants were the finest, and as for Yates—well, Everett Edward Yates was anything but an alarmist. In early manhood he had had a brilliant career as a corps commander under Sherman, during the Atlantic campaign of the Civil War. He emerged from the war to become chief surveyor, and then assistant engineer, of the Union Pacific Railway, under General Dodge. Stories of his bravery and honesty were legion—and true—involving his part in building the UP cross-country, in the face of marauding Indians, grafters, land grabbers, and highly placed political opportunists. Still in his forties, Yates had a distinguished reputation, and although Jessie had never met him, she knew of him very well.

Indeed, it was his name alone that had prompted Jessie to invest in Yates's latest venture. Striking out on his own, Yates was the promoter, financier, and developer of a short-line railroad, the Puget Sound & Cascade. It would, when—

and if—it was completed, connect Tacoma with the mountainous mining communities, ending somewhere near Stampede Pass. What made the venture so absurdly risky was that there was no mainline railroad to which the PS&C could join. But Yates was convinced that within a few years the Northern Pacific would finish building its route to the Columbia River, and then head up the Yakima Valley and tunnel through Stampede Pass. Then his PS&C would be a ready-constructed link that would net him and his backers a fortune.

The sheer audacity of Yates's gamble intrigued Jessica, but her main reason for investing was to get the PS&C as far as the Snowshoe. Ore wagons were better than nothing, but rail hoppers to a port like Tacoma would provide much more and cheaper transportation—and a much-needed boost to Snowshoe's profits. So, while she wasn't a heavy backer, she'd bought enough PS&C stock to show her interest. And now Yates was asking Jessie to prove her interest, without telling her what she might be buying into.

"Yates and his crews, as I told you, Ki, have always fought their own battles till now," Jessie reiterated. "Something mighty odd must be happening to make matters more than run-of-the-mill. Otherwise Yates never would have called on Starbuck for help."

Ki was in agreement with those words as he stood in the stirrups and stretched, to relieve his fatigue. Something unusual was astir, and he knew Jessie wouldn't rest until she discovered what.

He glanced around swiftly and surveyed the terrain. They were riding across a high mountain meadow filled with colorful Indian paintbrush, lupine, and a profusion of vines and ferns, angling toward a narrow pass where mossy rocks were piled high on either side. A short distance beyond this pass, he gathered, was the small mining town of Forge. It was there that they would stop, because Forge was where Yates had his current temporary headquarters, the PS&C railhead only a couple of miles past that.

It would have been nice, Ki mused, if they'd been able to ride the PS&C to Forge. But to have caught one of its work trains would have required a trek to Tacoma, which would have been just as long a jaunt as the one they were on. So, when they'd arrived in Seattle yesterday evening, they'd hired horses at a livery, slept over in a good hotel, and set off early this morning.

Their ride, at least, was a change of pace from the pitching coastal packet boat that had brought them up from Los Angeles, just as that had been different from the sooty train trip from El Paso to Los Angeles. Their horseback trek was a great deal slower, the trail they were following threading through increasingly difficult terrain of crags, crevices, and close stands of trees, passing innumerable streams and gulches, woodcutters' and trappers' claims, and half-hidden paths to isolated digs. And all the while Ki and Jessie had stayed in the saddle, eating only the cold food in their saddlebags.

Forge had damned well better lie just beyond the pass ahead, Ki concluded. And it had better have a restaurant that served hot meals, and a hotel with mattresses, too...

Jessie was inspecting the country around them too, and her sharp eyes saw nothing to arouse her suspicions. Nobody was in sight, either ahead of them or behind them, and the meadow was so open that there seemed no spot where a man might hunker in ambush. Still, she held the reins in her left hand, so that her right hand was free and near her revolver. Long ago she'd learned that there was always a chance it would be fatal to relax her vigilance, even in a place where there was apparently no danger.

They rode on slowly, side by side, as they approached

7

the mouth of the little pass. It was about a quarter of a mile long and appeared to open out into a broad field similar to the meadow they were leaving. While moving deeper within the confines of the pass, they were studiously surveying the jumbles of rock when abruptly something sounding like a hornet buzzed between them, almost brushing against Jessie's shoulder. From downwind came the crack of a rifle.

Instantly they sought cover, and had jumped their horses aside and forward with heels and reins when a second bullet seared the crown of Ki's rumpled hat. Shielded by a clump of boulders, they stopped and sprang out of their saddles, ground-hitching their half-spooked horses. Jessie's revolver was out of its holster as her boots hit the ground.

But no third shot came.

"Now what?" she asked grimly, peering ahead.

"Now it's to be a stalking party," Ki replied, hunkering beside her. "Somewhere in front of us is a man—or men— who fired without warning. Now they're trying to wait us out."

"But why? Are they after us, or did they mistake us for others?"

Ki shrugged. Regardless of the reason for the attack on them, it was a fact, and neither he nor Jessie had any intention of letting whoever had done it get away with it. It had been a plain attempt at bushwhack murder, and Jessie voiced their angry intentions when she answered her own question:

"Well, if we're going to find out why, we're going to have to head up and ask them. We certainly can't stay here."

Cautiously they began working their way up into the rocks, always keeping behind cover. They knew from which direction the shots had come, and that was all, but they wanted to get on higher ground, to try to be at least as high as the man or men in ambush.

8

A gentle breeze was soughing toward them, carrying sounds, and that was to their advantage. Ki thought he heard a boot scrape rock, and tensed. But it was Jessie who first spied a man moving stealthily out from cover and start toward a new position.

He never lived to reach it. Jessie's Colt bucked in her fist, and the man sprawled, then tumbled over the rocks to the trail below.

To Ki's ears the wind brought a muttered curse that did not come from the man Jessie had shot. "There's another one still hiding up ahead," he cautioned Jessie in a low, urgent tone. "Stay put and cover me. I'll see if I can't prod him into showing."

Silent and motionless, Jessie waited and watched while Ki eased slowly and cautiously to higher ground. Again he heard boots scraping against the rocks. Once more he tensed, listening intently, trying to gauge the second ambusher's position and distance.

The man was creeping closer, Ki realized, ready to fire upon sight of either one of them. And for all Ki knew, he might be a crack shot. The man was definitely trying to act like a snake, slithering and slouching behind the rocks, but he was nervous, edgy, not always placing his hard leather boots down as quietly as he should.

In such a situation it was understandable for men to grow nervous and twitchy. But Ki only grew more icy and calculating. He was hunting a callous bushwhacker, and he meant to use the same methods he would have employed in going after a vicious wild animal. Noiselessly he inched forward, his nimble fingers feeling the razorlike *shuriken* that were tucked in his vest pockets.

He heard the man grunt softly, and paused in a crouch, listening to the sounds the wind brought to his ears. Suddenly, then, he stood up, facing the man, who was less than thirty feet away. The man fired at virtually the same instant.

Ki twisted in a low, rolling circle, the bullet from the man's carbine ricocheting off stone between Ki's legs. The man couldn't lever and fire again, because by then several of the points of a glittering *shuriken* were protruding from his chest.

The man coughed, shaking from the impact of Ki's weapon. He dropped his carbine, which clattered down among the rocks, then sagged and sprawled.

Ki rose, prepared to hurl another *shuriken* if need be. A noise behind him made him spin around, but it was only Jessie, scrambling up with her revolver held ready, relief welling in her eyes.

"Thank God," she sighed tremulously. "Is he . . . ?"

"Not yet. But I'm pretty sure he's the last."

Jessie, training her revolver on the man, walked forward with Ki and stood over the prostrate, dying figure. "Why'd you open fire on us?" she demanded. "Who did you think we were?"

"Starbuck gal, ain't you?" the man gasped.

"Yes."

"That's who we thought you was . . ."

"Why? How'd you know we were coming this way?"

"We . . . knew."

"Who are you? Who was your partner?"

"Don't make no difference now . . ." The man choked, grimacing with pain. "You got him, and I'm slippin' fast. But there'll be others."

"So you were working for somebody who wanted me dead," Jessie said.

"Y-yeah . . ."

"Why not tell the whole thing?" she urged. The man was right; he was sinking fast. "You'll feel better if you get it off your conscience."

10

"The hell with you..."

That was the end. The man on the rocks shuddered and turned his head away. His chest heaved once and he was gone, his boots twitching a final, faint tattoo on the stony earth.

Perplexed, Jessie stared down at the corpse. She couldn't understand it, but there had been some sort of plot to waylay her here in this small pass, before she could reach Forge and learn why Yates had asked for help. Since she'd telegraphed back to expect her, and he hadn't mentioned any need for secrecy, she wasn't surprised that somebody else had found out she was coming. Probably everyone in and around Forge knew by now. It was just that this mysterious trouble was suddenly becoming grimmer and deadlier.

She turned and went to where Ki had recovered the man's rifle and was examining it. There was no mark on it to give them a clue. They looked around for horses, hoping a brand might hold a hint, but couldn't find any sign of them. The two men must either have hidden their mounts away from the pass, or left them to be watched by yet a third man.

Clambering down over the rocks, Jessie and Ki reached the floor of the pass, where the first man had landed on the trail. This hombre was also a stranger to them, and his carbine was also devoid of any identifying marks. The best they could come up with was that both men were middle-aged, nondescript, and traveling light. Probably hired gunmen, Jessie decided.

"Or outlaws, part of some gang," Ki suggested, as they remounted their horses. "Do you think the cartel is involved?"

"At this point, Ki, your guess is as good as mine. It sure smacks of their backshooting methods, though." Gathering up the reins, she rode slowly alongside Ki, watching carefully as they went on through the pass and emerged into open meadow again. "But if the cartel is behind this," she added, tight-lipped, "I'm going to fight it just the way I always have."

Hers was a lifelong fight, inherited by her, along with the rest of the Starbuck empire, at the death of her father. Alex Starbuck had begun the struggle when, as a young importer-exporter in the Orient, he'd run afoul of a powerful and unscrupulous cabal of Prussian entrepreneurs. In one of their strikes at him they murdered his lovely wife, Sarah, in an effort to scare him into silence; but their move backfired, as they shortly discovered, when Alex strangled the son of one of their leaders with his bare hands. Thus had the protracted war between Alex Starbuck and the cartel intensified. And as Alex became richer and more powerful, and could delve deeper into the workings of his enemies, he discovered that the cartel's main focus was on domination of the commercial and political life of the emerging United States.

Tragically, the cartel also became richer and more powerful, despite Alex Starbuck winning many a battle. Eventually he gave his own life to the war, when the cartel assassinated him from ambush on his own Circle Star Ranch. They'd underestimated Jessie, however, who by then had grown to be a shrewd, determined, beautiful woman, old enough to take her father's place.

Among other things to which Jessie fell heir was Alex Starbuck's secret notebook, in which he'd recorded detailed information about the cartel, its holdings and members. She'd used it to track his murderer—whom she'd repaid in kind. Ever since, relying on the continually updated ledger and aided by Ki and her own inherited wealth and influence, Jessie had continued her father's war, vowing never to cease until she or the cartel was dead, one or the other finally destroyed.

12

Nothing in the notebook or other reports had indicated that the cartel was involved in Yates's PS&C, or in the Snowshoe Mines. It didn't matter. When a man of the stature of E. E. Yates wanted help, help was what he was going to get.

Jessie touched her spurs to the flanks of her roan gelding. The town of Forge, according to her information, was only a few miles ahead. Once there, perhaps Yates could supply her with some reason for the trap in the pass.

She hoped so. She hated to fight blind.

Chapter 2

It proved to be more than a few miles ahead.

Dusk was flaming beyond the black crags of the distant Olympic Mountains when Jessie and Ki gigged their footsore mounts into the outskirts of Forge. What once had been a mundane mining settlement was now, thanks to construction of the PR&C, a rip-snorting end-of-track town. Of course, Forge paled in comparison to the utter lawlessness and depravity of earlier hells on wheels such as Julesburg, Cheyenne, Laramie, and Evanston, which were already becoming part of American folklore. Nevertheless, Jessie and Ki felt the impact of Forge's rowdy, bloody, brawling boom-camp spirit as they entered its ugly main street.

The recently laid PR&C tracks bisected the town, heading toward the far side, where the machine shops and temporary roundhouse were located. Sidetracks were occupied by seemingly endless rows of flatcars loaded with crossties and steel rails, barrels of spikes and crates of fishplates.

It was in that yonder section where Jessie felt she'd find E. E. Yates, parked near the action in his private day coach.

A different sort of action infested the town proper. The false fronts of saloons and honkytonks, gambling halls and dubious hotels bracketed the railroad line, etched against the sunset like the uneven battlements of a ruined castle. Even shabbier were the canvas tents and the soddies where saloonkeepers dispensed watered whiskey and marked cards, while barkers stood in front and shouted the questionable attractions of their establishments:

"C'mon, you sports! Our bar serves the finest rotgut in the West! Give our games a try! Git an honest deal!"

Along the street, the flotsam and jetsam of humanity rubbed shoulders in a constant flow back and forth, in and around. Gamblers in frock coats and painted hussies in crinoline were taking their sundown strolls before their night's work began. Buckskin-clad hunters and trappers; bearded lumberjacks and dirt-grimy miners; greenhorns fresh from the East to seek their fortunes—all jostled in converging streams as they headed for bars and poker tables. Burly spikers and graders and other railroad construction crewmen, sweat-stained from a hard day's toil, added to the noisy confusion.

Jessie and Ki worked their horses through the congested traffic. The street was without sidewalks, a river of dust that rose high to choke their nostrils and impede their vision. Yet, for all its uproar and crudeness, Forge's spirit laid its sharp edge against Jessie, quickening her heart with a sense of adventure. She drank in the myriad smells and sounds and sights, sensing the town's underlying drama, its crosscurrents of greed and jealousy and hate and sham love—

—Until, without warning, three galloping horses slewed around the corner ahead, directly into Ki's path. Two were

15

being ridden by a pair of young men in lumberjack clothes, their features so similar that they could have been taken for twins. The third horse, slightly in the lead, was being given loose rein and a heavy spurring by a solid, grizzled oldster with square features roughened and burned a deep red by constant exposure to the weather.

One of the boys gave a yelp of alarm and jerked his horse to the left, colliding with the other's mount and nearly causing a spill for both. But there was no time to prevent a collision between the white-haired man and Ki, though the man wrenched savagely on his reins.

As the man's snorting black stallion stiffened its legs to slide to a halt, Ki heeled his roan into a swift leap forward, putting all of the horse's weight into the meeting. The result of his split-second thinking was an instant reversal of advantage in the roan's favor. Its shoulder hit the black solidly in the ribs, and the black went down in a flurry of splayed hoofs. The man was hurled clear, and thudded into the dust of the street.

Immediately, Ki dismounted. He strode to the fallen man and extended a helping hand. But a deep furrow of rage had formed between the man's brows, and his heavy chest swelled with indignation, his thick pectoral muscles outlined beneath the soggy plaid cloth of his sweat-soaked shirt. He leaped to his feet, rasping curses, the fingers of his right hand forming a callused, gnarled fist that punched out wickedly at Ki's face.

Ki, standing eyeball-to-eyeball with the man, did not move his feet. He swayed gracefully aside, and the fist whizzed over his shoulder. Almost at the same instant, something like the slim steel end of a logging wedge took the man squarely on the angle of his jaw. The man lifted from his feet and landed back in the dust, and this time he stayed.

The two young men gave simultaneous yells of anger.

16

Their hands flashed for the worn grips of their pistols, which were stuck barrels-down in the waistbands of their pants. But even as they gripped their weapons, they froze grotesquely, their faces strained and whitening. They were staring into the unwavering black muzzle of Jessie's Colt revolver.

"One down," she said pleasantly, "and two to go."

"Uh-uh," one said, shaking his head hastily.

"We ain't feared of nothin' that walks, crawls, hops, or flies," the other said. "Nothin' 'cept women holdin' shootin' irons." And his hand, too, dropped from the pistol grip.

"Thanks, Jessie," Ki said, and turned to the boys. "I don't see any reason for getting riled over this. Simmer down."

The boys started to speak, but were interrupted by the older man, who was rising gingerly to his feet, rubbing his jaw. "Reckon the gent is right. 'Sides, we were to blame for the bust-up, not him." He glanced admiringly at Ki. "Feller, when you hit, you hit. No hard feelin's, though, and here's my hand on it. Name's Adams, Rufus Adams. And these are the Pace twins, Ian and Olin."

"Glad to know you," Ki acknowledged. "I'm called Ki, and this is Miss Jessie Starbuck."

They all shook hands gravely. One of the Pace twins opened his mouth to speak again, when Adams glanced over and gave a contemptuous snort. "Ah Lordy, we've woken up Sheriff Meek."

A stout, bandy-legged man was stomping toward them, his handlebar mustache bristling on his scarlet face. On his sagging vest gleamed a big nickel badge with SHERIFF engraved on its surface. He was wheezing loudly, evidently in bad temper, and halted directly in front of Adams and glared up belligerently.

"Awright, awright, you can't come barging into town

17

an' knock folks down. Not while I'm the law here, Rufus."

Adams's face wrinkled with a soulful expression. "Gawsh, Meek, I'm plumb sorry. I must've been bad mistook about it."

"About what?"

"Why, knocking this gent down. I thought I did, but if you says I can't do that, I reckon I must be mistook."

The sheriff began sputtering. "Y-you listen here—"

"Naw, you listen. This gent and me smoked the pipe, and everything's cinched up proper." Adams, now grinning maliciously, poked his forefinger into the sheriff's vest. "If'n you want to get wringy about something, go tackle them Red Devils."

"I have been, an' most all of last night, too," Meek retorted stoutly. "After dark, they cut loose over at the railhead, just as an engine was pullin' a crane into position."

"And?"

"Four of the night crew were wounded and one killed. Plus, them skunks managed to lob enough blasting powder to bust the engine and crane to smithereens. Soon's I heard, I mounted a posse."

"And?"

"We lost them," Meek admitted, deflating a little. "Down near Green River. That's one of the cussedest sections around."

"It's a stretch, I grant you. But I hazard they could drive a buffalo across a snowbank and leave you behind."

"Now see here, Adams, you ain't got no call to—"

"Do you have much of that kind of trouble hereabouts?" Jessie asked, hastily cutting in on the irate sheriff's bellow.

He turned to answer her. "Too blamed much during the last year, ever since those danged Red Devils started hittin' this area."

"Who are they?"

18

"Nobody knows for positive, 'cept they're an owlhoot bunch led by Red Duvall, whoever he is. Duvall, Devil, you get it? Anyway, ma'am, they been robbin' and wide-loopin' and the like, but mainly they been raisin' hob with the new railroad."

"Suits me fine," Adams interjected firmly.

Meek gave the old lumberman a caustic glance. "Huh! Rufus here, he ain't got no more use for the railroad than the Red Devils do, but he objects to it only out of sheer contrariness," the sheriff explained to Jessie. "Point being, though, the Red Devils almost have the construction crew too jumpy to work. Anybody who's a redhead comes under powerful suspicion, as you can imagine, even though half the Irishers on the crew are growin' carrots for hair. But I'll nail 'em yet. They've had all the breaks so far, but the time'll come when they'll slip or their luck'll run out."

"Well, I ain't holding my breath," Adams cracked, then motioned to the Pace twins. "C'mon, boys, let's twine our nags and go order the supplies."

"Let's drop over to the Black Nugget for a drink first," Ian Pace suggested, and Olin chimed in, "For eats, too. I'm so hungry my belly thinks my throat's been slit."

Adams shook his head. "No, not for me on this trip. I've got too much work to lollygag in town, boys, but you can go ahead if you like. Just make it back to camp by dawnin', y'hear?" Adams then nodded to Jessie and Ki. "Drop in on us if you happen our way, up along Moon Trail Canyon. S'long."

As Adams and the Pace brothers began walking their horses toward a convenient hitching rail, Sheriff Meek remarked sourly, "He seldom comes to Forge, but by jimmies, seldom is too often."

Jessie smiled wryly. "I gather that Mr. Adams isn't very popular with you?"

"Rufus don't take enough dallies on his temper, and is always goin' off half-cocked. When he's loggin', he expects freighters ahead of everyone else. When he stays over, he demands the best room at the Black Nugget, a private card game in back of its saloon, and Nanette Thrall to entertain only him. Popular with *me?* Ma'am, there wouldn't be three mourners if Rufus was to be put in a coffin and buried tomorrow."

Adams, having tethered his horse, was angling across the crowded street toward a large general store. The twins were entering a saloon whose doorway resounded with alcohol-fed noise, and whose windows were dusty-paned but blazing golden. The saloon comprised one half of a long, two-story tandem building. Coal-tar torches illuminated a sign painted above a wooden awning that made a series of swaybacked scallops along the veranda-style porch: BLACK NUGGET HOTEL & CLUB.

"I think it'd be faster to walk than to ride," Jessie commented to Ki, glancing about at the roiling throngs. "It'd probably do us good to stretch our legs, anyway. Let's tie up."

Ki nodded, and searched for an empty spot at the packed hitch rails that fronted the main street buildings. At first it seemed as though Adams and the twins had found the last to be had, but finally he spotted an opening at the hotel's rack. Gathering the reins of both horses, he started thrusting toward it.

Jessie fell in behind him. So did Sheriff Meek.

"If you're stayin' over, your best bet's the Black Nugget," Meek told Jessie. "A new place. Fellers by the names of Latwick and Chaber opened it up just before the railroad decided to build thisaway. They must've had some inside information. Folks were sorta flabbergasted when they set up business—Hilliard Latwick handling the hotel half and George Chaber the saloon—but right off came the an-

20

nouncement that the road was a-comin' on through."

Jessie listened to the gabby sheriff with interest, wanting as much information as she could get about the town and its people. She had to strain to hear him, though. Her ears rang from the din of carousers, barkers, off-key music, the shrill laughter of women.

"Yeah, the Black Nugget sure caught our ol' reg'lar places flatfooted," Meek rambled on. "'Tain't cheap or tawdry, either. Chaber hired Nanette Thrall to handle his dancin' gals, and Nanette don't tolerate any monkeyshines. No matter what gamblin', drinkin', or brawlin' is happenin' at the bar, the gals have to behave on the floor or they're out. That goes for their rooms in back, and the hotel part too. No drinkin', no sportin', no roughhousin'.'"

"Remarkable. And Chaber agrees with such strictness?"

"I dunno how much he agrees, but he has to put up with it or lose Nanette. 'Sides, it don't appear to be hurtin' him any. You can see for yourself that his saloon's so jammed it's buzzin' like a bottle full o' bees." The sheriff nudged Jessie, and indicated a man stepping outside. "Look, there's Chaber now. Right pert-lookin' jasper, don't you think?"

Jessie had to agree. George Chaber presented a fashion-plate image; he was a tall and leonine man somewhere in his late thirties, who moved with supple grace and projected a healthy outdoors look.

Chaber hesitated by the end-post of the overhanging porch, lit a cheroot, then nodded affably as another man approached him.

Lamplight from the saloon windows illuminated the second man when he stopped to converse with Chaber. Jessie could see that he had a lean, swarthy face with a prominent, high-bridged nose, a hard mouth, and conspicuous cheekbones. His hair was dark brown, and was styled with short sideburns that blended into a bushy but well-barbered mustache and full General Grant beard.

21

"That's Woodrow Fleishman," the sheriff observed. "We call him Woody, natch'rally. He migrated up here eight or nine months ago, all the way from Calexico and that there border country. Set up a haulin' business, and just when it looked like the railroad would be puttin' him under, he wangled a contract with 'em to freight stuff across to where they're cuttin' ahead of the tracks. Woody is smart. Funny sort of cuss, though. Him and his teamsters stick together and don't mix much. They're quiet, no trouble, and they hold their drink, but most of 'em pack guns under their coats, and I've a notion they could be plenty salty if necessary."

A burst of gunshots and a high-pitched scream lanced through the noise around them. It was followed almost instantly by confused shouts and trampling boots, as men up by the hotel end of the Black Nugget backed hurriedly from the mouth of an alleyway.

"Somethin's busted loose!" Sheriff Meek barked, drawing his revolver while sprinting toward the scene of the commotion.

Jessie and Ki tagged after him. Now others began converging on the alley, curiosity luring them from the street and saloons, and they crowded around, babbling with alarm, as the trio reached the alley. It was a very narrow and black-shadowed path that stretched rearward along the sides of the hotel and the adjoining building, but where it opened onto the street lay the sunset-dappled body of a man, face downward in the dust.

"Not again," the sheriff growled, kneeling beside the fallen man. He turned him over on his back and stared at the blood-streaked face. "Glory be, it's Roland, the railroad's assistant superintendent of construction!" he snapped, then glared into the alley. "He must've been drygulched from in there."

Ki, also giving the alley a quick look, suddenly leaped aside and shoved the sheriff down, hands streaking for his vest. At the same instant a stream of gunfire blasted from the black depths of the alley. Ki winced as a bullet slashed his left forearm.

The sheriff yelled with startled pain as another bullet flecked a patch of skin from the end of his nose. He yelled again as Jessie, standing on the other side of the alley mouth, triggered her revolver three times in rapid succession, sweeping the alley left, right, and center with an answering hail of lead.

Thumb hooked over the hammer of her custom Colt, Jessie listened intently, deafened for the moment by the roar of her own pistol. She heard a pounding of footsteps receding into the alley. Then she glimpsed Ki bounding to his feet and, weaving and ducking, racing in pursuit.

Diving after the fleeing killer, Ki was perhaps a score of yards inside the alley when something caught him a terrific blow just below the knees. He sailed through the air, fighting reflexively to regain his balance. Twisting, he curled his lithe body into a roll, and instead of landing with a breath-jarring thud, he came out of his roll virtually on his feet again.

Instinctively he shifted position, thinking he heard a sound farther down the alley. Clasping a small handful of *shuriken* the way a gambler would deal a deck of cards, he sent a couple winging toward the sound. Then he crouched, waiting.

All was silent, save for the voices of Sheriff Meek and the bystanders at the mouth of the alley. He heard the sheriff's boots pounding toward him, and his wheezing breath.

"Careful!" Ki warned loudly. "There's a rope stretched across the alley."

He heard the sheriff yelp, fall heavily in a belly-flop,

23

and swear lustily as he picked himself back up. There was a note of injured pride in the lawman's profanity which caused Ki to chuckle. Pocketing his unused *shuriken*, he drifted quietly along the alley on the chance that he had downed one of the ambushers. But he found nothing, the rest of the alley and the trash-strewn field behind the buildings being completely deserted. Beyond the field were a few dark hovels and a great many trees. Nothing stirred.

"Not a trace," he reported, returning to the sheriff.

"Nervy sidewinders," Meek growled. He was still by the rope, stooping as he rubbed his bruised shins. "Waited after they'd gunned that pore feller, and hey, looks like they got you!"

"Nothing much," Ki replied as they walked back toward the alley entrance. "Has Forge got a doctor?"

"Not to spare on flesh wounds, we don't. See Martha." The sheriff glanced back, commenting, "They fixed that rope aforehand, for their getaway. Figured anyone goin' in would fall over it."

Ki nodded in reply and asked, "Who's Martha?"

Before the sheriff could answer, one of the gawkers around the construction superintendent yelled out, "Hey, c'mere, Sheriff! Roland ain't dead yet, but he's hurt mighty bad. Hole in his head."

"That'd do it," the sheriff allowed, as he and Ki hastened up. He hunkered down for a swift examination, while Ki went and calmly assured Jessie that his wound was only a scratch needing a bandage strip, which he'd have done as soon as he learned who and where someone named Martha was.

The sheriff rose, concluding, "He's meat for Doc Elgin, but I dunno how well Roland will take to being hauled feedsack style."

Chaber, the saloon owner, wedged forward and suggested, "Rig a stretcher. I've got some mop poles we can

24

use." He turned to the man right beside him, who was wearing a miner's outfit, complete to laced boots and stiff-brimmed Stetson. "Ted, would you mind fetching them? You know where the mops are kept, don't you?"

"Yeah, yeah, back o' the bar," the man replied, his voice slurring as if he'd imbibed a drink too many. He was lanky and young, his face tanned and pleasant enough, except for a bleariness to his eyes and a slightly petulant pout to his mouth. He started thrusting through the crowd. "I'll be back in a flash, George."

Jessie glanced at Ki, cocking an eyebrow, then asked Chaber, "Is that Ted Baldwin of the Snowshoe Mines?"

Chaber nodded, smiling perfunctorily at her, and shifted to get a better view of the wounded man's face. "Roland makes the count five now—or is it six? They're adding up fast, Oswald."

Sheriff Meek grimaced, either from Chaber's observation or from the use of his first name. "Uh-huh, six, all of 'em key men in the railroad's organization. At this rate they'll never get the road built. Yates will have a stroke when I tell him about this."

"We were on our way to see Mr. Yates," Jessie said. "If you prefer, Sheriff, we could break the news to him for you."

"Thanks kindly, much obliged." Meek scratched his jaw and let out a deep sigh. "Sure wish someone could tell Yates what he'll really want to hear. Who did it."

The sheriff's query caused a curious hush. Men glanced at one another, but apparently no one saw fit to reply until Ted Baldwin, returning with two mop poles, elbowed to the front.

"Coupla guesses," he declared, sounding as if he'd taken an extra drink along with the poles. "The Red Devils, for one."

"And the other?" Meek asked.

Baldwin shrugged. "I ain't naming names till I'm sure," he responded, handing over the poles. "By the bye, where's Rufus Adams? Didn't he hit town just a jiffy ago?"

Sharp, angry shouts erupted from the Pace twins, and they shoved through to confront Baldwin. "You don't mean you're accusin' our boss of havin' something to do with this?" Olin demanded.

Baldwin regarded both boys coldly. "You're the ones bringing that subject up."

Olin flushed darkly, and Ian dipped his hand toward his pistol butt. Ted Baldwin swayed boozily but otherwise did not move. His challenging eyes didn't waver from their faces. But Jessie caught a peripheral glimpse of Chaber flexing his fingers, spreading them clawlike. Simultaneously the saloon owner's left hand almost casually caressed the left lapel of his long black coat. Chaber was a shoulder-holster man, she realized, recognizing the gesture of the gunman who swings his coat aside to draw from the armpit. And she was willing to give odds that he was fast and deadly.

With apparent thoughtlessness, she stepped between the Pace brothers and Ted Baldwin. "Who'll volunteer his coat to make the stretcher?" she asked brightly. "We must save Mr. Roland."

George Chaber smiled thinly, and there was almost an amused expression in his cool, composed eyes. Ian Pace moved his hand away from his pistol, and his brother grunted something under his breath. Baldwin visibly relaxed, grinning as a number of men offered their coats.

Sheriff Meek supervised construction of the stretcher until Jessie interrupted him to say, "We're going now, to see Mr. Yates."

"*You're* going now, Jessie," Ki corrected her. "I'll go later, after the sheriff directs me to Martha's place."

The sheriff tweaked his mustache. "Fancy me, an' I assumed everyone knew Martha's. She's up 'cross the street in rooms over the druggist. Take the side steps and knock." He returned just in time to coordinate the sliding of mop poles through the sleeves of a coat.

Ki left then, wending his way up the congested street. Jessie eyed him for a moment, concerned but not distressed. Ki didn't lean toward either histrionics or martyrdom, so when he claimed his wound was minor and needed only a bandage, Jessie took his word for it. And now she saw he'd gone out of sight.

Jessie wheeled around to go down the main street—and was bumped lightly, accidentally, by a stretcher man. Sheriff Meek glanced sidelong at her. "You're not waiting for your friend, are you?"

"I'm on my way to Mr. Yates, as you know. I've no intention of waiting, and if I had, I've no reason to. Ki got hardly more than a scratch, and I'm sure your nurse can clean and bandage it just fine. The town must find her handy, living over the druggist."

With a slight shrug, the sheriff turned to resume managing, only to see Supervisor Roland already lifted and lying ready on the stretcher. "Nice work, boys, now let's go, afore this feller cashes in." And then Meek called to Jessie, as she was going, "Sure, a nurse! Martha's known for curing what ails . . ."

The druggist's building resembled most of the other dilapidated buildings along the street, except for the crude block-lettered DRUGS across its front window. There was no other sign or illustration. Inside was a ramshackle shop looking as unsavory as any rotgut dive, and patronized by much the same sort of rowdies and laborers.

Ki caught all this while passing the front of the shop,

27

after checking the near alley and finding no outside steps. So he strolled by the entrance, where mean laughter and spasmodic profanities flowed through the open doorway, and continued up to the far corner, where a narrow alleyway went alongside to the building's rear.

He cut into the alley, and after a few yards he came to a steep, rickety staircase that led to a second-floor landing. Up there, Ki figured, in something like a loft over the druggist's, would be where this Martha most likely lived.

He started up the stairs, not trying to be sneaky-quiet, but not trying to make his slippers sound like boots, either. He could see, after climbing some steps, that on the landing was a door, and next to it a curtained window. There was no light behind the window, no sound either, and this made him believe Martha was out. When he got to the landing he discerned that the curtain was more of a drape, overlapping the window frame and blotting out any light.

He eased up against the door, listening. The silence was intense, so intense that he got suspicious. It was as if there was a hush inside there, trying too hard to be a complete silence.

So. Ki backed and considered carefully: *The house is likely empty. If Martha is there, she doesn't wish to be disturbed.* Anyway, there were others who could bind his arm, maybe in the drug shop. Besides, he should quietly leave precisely because he didn't want to, because he hated to turn down a challenge, especially when it was as silly and irritating as this. He should build character with it instead.

Later, he told himself, and started beating his right fist on the door. No shouting, no kicking, only his fist pounding the crap out of the door. It took a couple of minutes, but then he heard the padding of feet.

"Who's that?" asked a sharp female voice.

"Martha? Are you Martha? I was told to see you."

"Kee-rist, don't you fellows ever give up?"

"Look, Martha, I don't know what you're talking about. I'm a stranger in Forge, and Sheriff Meek told me to see you about—"

"Oooh, sure he did!" She made a derisive snort. "I almost fell for your line there, bucko. Now go away, y'hear?"

He wondered what ailed her. "Martha, let me in! I'm hurt!"

Silence. Utter, implacable silence.

"It's true, Martha. I'm wounded, just—"

"We all have our share of broken hearts, bucko, so suffer."

"Not that kind! I've got a flesh wound. I'm bleeding on your landing. My name is Ki, I was sent by Meek. Please let me in."

"I most certainly will not."

"I'll throw a rock through the window."

The inside bolt shot back. Martha opened the door like a gust of wind, and looked at Ki half in dismay, half in defiance.

"Evening," Ki said cheerily. "Will you bandage my arm?"

"I'm alone. But don't let my nightgown fluster you too much."

"I wouldn't care if you were naked," Ki said, stepping inside. "I'm here to talk business about my arm."

Martha, who'd been closing the door, now swung it wide again. "Out! I see, now, that it was a trick all along, to get in my house and good graces!" She planted two fists on her hips, her breasts swelling beneath her floor-length Mother Hubbard. Martha was in her late twenties, with auburn hair on the dark side, a well-rounded nose and chin, and a full ruby mouth. Eyes that were a very pale violet, and stripes in the Mother Hubbard to match. A fine gown, Ki thought, and a fine lot of female in it.

"I've no intention of leaving, Martha, so close the door. It took me half your tantrum to figure out your meaning, and if you'd like to know my meaning, just take a look at the floor."

Martha slammed the door and looked. "Blood. So?"

"My blood, Martha. It's coming from my left arm! Don't you see? I came here to get bound up!"

"Oh no, I'm out of them perversions, too. I know a rope lady—"

"My arm, Martha. If you can, take care of my arm."

Martha gazed at the gashed arm, and the shredded shirtsleeve and blotches of spreading blood that covered him. "Well, I suppose even a condemned man deserves to be cared for."

She led him to a plain, square kitchen table and sat him down in a chair. A kettle stood on the stove, and from it she poured water into a basin and brought it to the table along with a jar of iodoform powder and a few clean rags. Using a sharp kitchen knife, she cut away the left sleeve of his shirt, and then she bathed the wound. Ki noted with surprise and some pleasure that her touch, for all her gruff manner, was gentle.

When she'd poured the iodoform on the wound and bound it, she surveyed her handiwork and said with a sense of satisfaction, "There. You can pour out the water in the alley."

Ki picked up the basin and carried it to the door, taking a look around as he did so. The room was, as he'd assumed, single and square, but with a corner alcove above the bed. A Henry rifle stood by the door, and on a peg above it hung a scuffed gunbelt and holster holding an old thumb-buster Colt.

When he returned to the table with the basin, she was

looking at him with a peculiar, quizzical expression. "Set down a minute," she said.

He did so. They'd been conversing throughout the time she'd been dressing his wound, mostly just to fill the air. Martha hadn't divulged much in the way of personal history, just enough for Ki to gather that for a short, desperately hungry stretch of her life she'd worked as a whore, had run with a few small gangs, and had thus come to know a good many men on both sides of the law—which, Ki assumed, was why Sheriff Meek had sent him to her. She was a good woman.

She continued to stare at him without speaking. As Ki reached into a trouser pocket for a half-eagle to pay her for her nursing services, she stood and stretched out a hand and placed her palm against his cheek and stroked it gently. She said, "When I rub down, it's smooth, and when I rub up, you've got whiskers."

He reared back a bit, surprised.

She laughed throatily. "I'm not that bad, y'know." She sidled closer and caressed her fingers along his bare chest. "I know what I said at first, and you can't think I'm truly that dumb. Call it passing a few hoops, to see where you're right for jumping after that. Not many men make it now, believe me. It's okay if you want me. I'm a woman, you're a man . . . aren't you?"

It was that last, that purring jab of hers, that got to Ki. A lot had happened today, and he was rightfully ready for sleep, but he guessed that was what made the difference between the sexes.

Ki played his hand along her thigh. The muscles of her leg tightened, and Martha stopped caressing his chest and stared down at his hand as he stroked her thigh.

"I don't feel so brave about this as I did," she said with

31

a sigh. "I really don't know you, don't know you at all."

"You started this."

"And you're different." She stopped talking and put her hand over his and played with his fingers, then placed them on her breast. She was going on with it, Ki knew then, and she said, "But if I knew how you'd be different, that'd spoil it."

Using his other hand, Ki untied the ribbon at the neck of her gown.

Martha shrugged the garment off and let it blossom down around her feet.

She was naked before him, her body firm and quite broad for a woman, tapering to a slim waist and then rounding out again in slim, strong hips. Her long thighs curved into well-formed legs.

Ki was impressed, and hastened to be rid of his clothes. Martha watched him tug off his boots and jeans. Then she led him to her unmade alcove bed.

They stretched out close alongside each other, and Ki glided his hand down over the smoothness of her buttocks. She raised her face and pressed her open mouth tightly against his, her hand searching down between them. He couldn't help gasping as her fingers closed around his shaft, and he ground his pelvis into her, pulling her beneath him. She opened her legs to accept him between them, and he plunged deep into her soft flesh.

"This is nice," she sighed, straining back against him.

Ki thought it was pretty good, too. He could feel her body throb as she undulated her hips against him, her thighs pressing against his legs as her ankles snaked over and locked around his calves.

Ki kept her too busy to talk for the next few minutes. When she did open her mouth, it was to sing out her delight, her arms wrapping tightly around his back, pulling him down against her breasts, her body following his rhythm in wild abandon. Her nails began digging at his flesh spasmodically, slithering down to knead and claw at the flesh of his pumping buttocks.

More frenzied now, Martha locked her ankles firmly around him, her naked flesh slippery from the sweat of her burgeoning passion. Arching her back, she pumped up and down, undulating slowly at first, then faster and faster, until finally every sensation surging within their bodies was expelled, and they collapsed, satiated.

After a moment Ki rolled away from her, and she moved up to prop her back against the head of the bed. "You're a strange one, y'know."

She was in a thoughtful, pensive position, her back against the headboard and her knees raised before her breasts.

"A very strange one," she repeated reflectively.

Ki slid his hand up her leg. She quivered and pinched her thighs together in a defensive gesture. Chuckling, Ki removed his hand and eased gingerly off the bed. "I'd like to stay," he said, smiling while he dressed. "I shouldn't have stayed as long as I have."

"Stick a second longer," she told him, yawning and rolling from the bed. She didn't retrieve her gown, but padded naked and unselfconsciously across the room to a chest of drawers, where she began rummaging through its contents.

Except for a shirt, Ki was dressed when Martha finished her hunt—which was for a shirt that fit him quite well. "Before... well, just before, Ki, was someone I'd known a long time, and I don't think we ever did get our things separated proper."

They went to the door together. Ki said, "I'd like to come back, Martha, but I don't know if I can... or when."

A slight, ironic smile creased her face. "If you knew how many men have said the same thing to me. And meant it, oh, and meant it." She stretched up and kissed him. "If I'm not here, I'll be somewhere else you'll visit. In that sense I'm always here."

Ki descended the stairs and hurried along the alley to the street. He was late, but it had been worth every minute of it.

Chapter 3

The railroad yard was clamorous with activity, its night crew busily preparing for the next day's labors. Chuffing work engines were shunting supplies for delivery to railend, and the roundhouse sheds reverberated from the clang of heavy repairs. Yet the yard itself was relatively small, and Jessie had little difficulty in locating Yates's personal day coach on a sidetrack near the stubby new depot.

Lights glowed in the coach, and posted by the steps at both ends were placards reading PRIVATE. Ignoring the notices, she climbed to the iron-railed front platform and rapped on the door. After a short delay it was opened by a short, ferret-eyed man wearing dark trousers and a sleeve-gartered shirt.

"Mr. Yates?" Jessie asked.

"No, Mr. Yates is busy." The man started closing the door. "You'll have to have an appointment. Come back tomorrow."

"I'm expected," she countered testily, wedging her foot in the doorway. "Tell Mr. Yates that Miss Starbuck has arrived."

"Very well." The man relinquished his hold on the door and gestured for her to enter. "Wait here, and I'll see."

"Here" proved to be the forward compartment of the austerely appointed coach. The man went through a connecting door, and a moment later he returned, accompanied by an imposingly tall and broad-shouldered man.

"Ah, my dear Miss Starbuck! At last we meet," the big man said, his movements quick and decisive as he approached and took her hand in a warm grip. His eyes held only friendliness, but the first man's were narrowed warily. The large man chuckled. "You'll have to excuse Virgil, I'm afraid. Like every good aide, he doesn't trust anybody. At times I believe he's even suspicious of me."

"I can't understand how, Mr. Yates."

"Everett, I insist. No sense in standing on stuffy formalities in such a forsaken spot as Forge," Yates replied genially, escorting her through the connecting door. "Or may I be so bold?"

"My friends call me Jessie."

"Consider me your friend." Yates shut the door, leaving Virgil looking irritated in the forward compartment. This, the rear section, appeared to be Yates's living quarters and office on wheels, with a bunk and washstand along one side, and a flat table, a set of filing cabinets, and some hard-backed chairs along the other. The table was a compost heap of charts and relief maps, looseleaf binders and odd stacks of ledgers; otherwise the compartment was more or less orderly, in a bachelor's sort of fashion.

In the same manner, Yates lacked the immaculate elegance of George Chaber. He was dressed in an expensive cutaway summer suit that was wrinkled from usage, a similarly wrinkled white shirt, and a black string tie that was knotted askew. His complexion was as fair as that of a Norseman, his hair rather blond, with just a hint of gray at the temples to make him look distinguished, not old. He was clean-shaven, with eyes as blue as a mountain lake, and a jutting jaw that implied a bit of ruthlessness, should the occasion demand it.

Jessie was impressed. If she were forced to choose between Yates and the exquisite saloon owner, she knew she'd pick Yates, wrinkles and all. He was not only a man's man, but a woman's man as well.

After mentioning that her friend, Ki, was to join them shortly, she immediately informed Yates of the tragic ambush of his superintendent, Roland.

"I'm shocked but not surprised," Yates responded, appearing more enraged than anything else. "Where is he? When can I see him?"

"He was taken to Dr. Elgin's. But he was unconscious, and I imagine he'll remain so for quite some time. I'm not sure there's anything you could do for him just yet, anyway."

Yates started pacing up and down the car, hands clasped behind his back. Then he began to speak. "It was going along pretty nicely up to about a year ago. Then my trains began being wrecked, my camps raided, jobs bungled, machinery sabotaged, my men slain in cold blood. It's become a virtual reign of terror."

"The Red Devils?"

"So you've heard of Duvall and his gang. Yes, Jessie, as far as I can tell, it's entirely their handiwork. I've had my share of trouble with bandits before, but never like this."

"But why? The PS&C isn't carrying anything valuable."

"It's carrying the railroad." Yates paused, picking up a black brier pipe and tamping in blacker tobacco. "My railroad, and the people it's certain to bring, will also mean the coming of true law and order. It'll put a stop to gangs like the Red Devils, and in my opinion, they're trying to stop me first."

"What about the sheriff?"

"The sheriff has been riding circles around himself, and getting nowhere." Yates struck a match, puffed a few times, and regarded Jessie. "That's why I'm so pleased you responded to my cable. I didn't anticipate you personally, of course, but with the resources of your Starbuck organization marshaled behind me, I feel we can root out those Devils before they cripple me completely."

"Everett, I appreciate your confidence in us. But we may not be able to do any more than the people who live here and are familiar with the mountains. Maybe not as much."

"Maybe not," Yates admitted, exhaling a cloud of acrid smoke. "On the other hand, some of the locals must be aiding and abetting the Devils, and who's to tell which ones. A few of them are openly against the railroad, and are causing me as many headaches as if they were part of the gang." Abruptly, Yates went to the table, dug out a detailed map of the area, and spread it flat. "For example, I've had plenty of boundary trouble with a forester named Rufus Adams. He claims his property overlaps land filed on by the railroad, and the old coyote has refused us right-of-way."

Poorly contoured, the map gave Jessie little sense of terrain detail, so she had to ask instead of read the obvious solution: "You've considered laying your track around Adams's property?"

"The only alternative would be a loop thirty-five miles long, and it's not even feasible from an engineering standpoint. We don't have the money, anyway. The PS&C is largely financed by local capital, raised by the lumbermen

38

and mine owners—such as yourself, Jessie—who'll be served by the line. We've lost more to the Red Devils than we can afford, and the vast majority of my backers have just about scraped the bottom of their wallets." Yates tapped the map with his pipestem. "No, our only possible route to Stampede Pass is through Baldwin's Moon Trail Canyon."

"Baldwin!" Jessica exclaimed. "I thought you said the property was owned by Adams."

"It is. Slip of the tongue, Jessie, sorry. Zack Baldwin used to own Moon Trail, but shortly before he passed away, he sold it to Adams. But listen, Jessie, if it's all the same, I really would like to go check on how Roland is doing. I'm sorry I'll be missing your friend this way, but I feel . . . well, responsible."

"You're not, Everett, but I understand. Ki will too."

Yates rolled up the map, and they left the rear compartment. Virgil was still in the forward section, perusing some documents, and seemed almost reluctant to leave when Yates told him he could call it a night. All three stepped from the coach, Yates locking the door behind them. Virgil angled off toward the roundhouse, while the others headed toward town.

While walking through the yard, Jessie said conversationally, "Moon Trail Canyon . . . an odd name."

"It came about because most of the rides through it were done by moonlight," Yates explained. "It's sort of a gateway between Green River Gorge and Stampede Pass, and shady folks used it to sift over the Cascades, both coming and going."

"If it's an old outlaw path, it can't be very wide."

"Plenty wide, Jessie, for a thirty-foot strip of railroad right-of-way. Freightwagons are using the trail right now— wagons, I might add, that we've had to contract for at fifty cents per load, thanks solely to Adams's hardheadedness."

"It seems to me you should sue, Everett. You should go to court and have Moon Trail Canyon condemned under public domain."

"We started to, but Adams blocked that by filing on Zack Baldwin's old mineral claim there. One thing's led to another—"

"Like to your freightwagon contract," she noted dryly.

"Yes, like to that. Woody Fleishman owns the wagons, and any delay is to his advantage. But what he'll lose directly when our road is built, I expect he'll pick up by short-trip deliveries of the stuff we'll be hauling. He's planning on it, too. But he's smart enough to keep on the good side of Adams."

"Sort of playing both ends against the middle."

"That's right, and figuring to win no matter which way the cat jumps. Woody is a sharp businessman. He agrees with me that the road going through will end the Red Devils, and that'll help honest enterprise."

"True enough," Jessie agreed thoughtfully. "Meanwhile, you're stymied by the Devils and Adams. Do you think they're tied in?"

"Could be, but I doubt it. Adams is too ornery to be partners for long with anybody. He swears that trains will ruin his peace and harm his precious timber. That's absurd. I suspect his real reason for fighting us is the same as for his filing on that claim. He's after the big, fat deposit of coking coal that Zack Baldwin always believed was under that canyon."

"Baldwin's son, Ted, I'm curious about him. And why you included Snowshoe in your wire," Jessie was saying, while they veered toward the Black Nugget to avoid a string of cargo wagons.

Once past the wagons, though, they saw Ki walking their way at a determined, long-striding clip. "My friend," Jessie explained. They slowed, waiting for him to approach, Jessie seeing quite enough to prompt her to greet him: "Heavens, you look worse for the cure!"

"Well, I feel great," Ki assured her, and after she introduced him to Yates, he added, "This is handy. I was just coming to see you."

"How's the arm now?"

"All patched. She did a fine job, one of the best. I'm sorry I'm late, but something unexpected came up."

Jessie felt a hunch that something had, indeed. "Not at all, Ki, what's important is you got taken care of properly. It's rare these days to find a nurse who'll give you the shirt off her back."

"Isn't it?" Ki agreed blandly, and as they moved toward the Black Nugget again, he turned to Yates and remarked, "Now, knowing Jessie, I'm sure I interrupted talk. Serious talk, that is."

"She was curious about Ted Baldwin and why I mentioned Snowshoe in my telegram," Yates answered, and shifted to include Jessie as he continued, "Nothing curious about Ted, 'cept he drinks and gambles and lets the mines go to pot. Ted's kind of wild when he gets to drinking. You're right, Jessie, he does carry a grudge, but it doesn't rear up much unless he's wallowing in a big snootful of red-eye. Swears he'll kill Adams some day, and everyone fears he's just man enough to try it."

"Killing doesn't take courage," Ki said. "Even the worst coward can pull a trigger, and is often the first to do so."

"Not against Rufus Adams. That old man is a ringtailed wampus, and one of the best shots in the Northwest. Funny about him. Only person he could ever get along with was Zack, but even that friendship was phony. For years he bankrolled Zack, first to buy the land, and then while Zack wore himself out hunting the coal. Sucked Zack so deeply

41

in debt to him that Zack had to deed the canyon to Adams to pay off."

"So that's why the boy hates him," Jessie said, as they passed the saloon and approached the hotel. "Ted thinks Adams swindled his father, and figures the coal belongs to him."

"Right you are, and nobody blames young Baldwin much. Since Zack died and Ted took over managing the Snowshoe, your mine had been going downhill steadily. And now this filing on his daddy's mineral claim. No wonder Ted's gone on the prod. I would myself."

"But you wouldn't get drunk and forget your job, Everett," Jessie replied tersely. "That's the difference. Ted may be using it as his excuse, but it's still no reason to fall apart."

There was a knot of men before the hotel lobby door—miners, lumberjacks, a few of the townsfolk. They were grouped around a fat, florid-faced man with a bulbous nose and thinning hair; and from their comments it was obvious they were not exactly pleased. Curious, Jessie, Ki, and Yates paused to listen.

The fat man, spotting Yates, called to him, "Is that correct, Ev? Did Rufus stop you again by filing on Zack's old claim?"

"Afraid so, Hilliard," Yates answered, and Jessie guessed that the fat man must be Hilliard Latwick, George Chaber's partner.

"Might have knowed the buzzard would do that," one of the men growled to his neighbor. "But damned if I can savvy why."

"Pure spite, Jake," said his companion, obviously a miner. "Ol' Baldwin would spin in his grave if Adams ever struck his coal."

A third man chimed in, "Gawd knows, Zack spent a heap o' time and cash tryin' to find it, before he gave over his land to Adams."

"That's another thing I don't understand," Jake said. "Don't reckon young Ted ever got it straight, either."

"You think there was something crooked about it, Ulrich?" Latwick asked. "I mean, more crooked than it already appears?"

"I wouldn't know, Mr. Latwick," Jake Ulrich replied, then turned to his miner pal. "You oughta know if anyone would. You work at the Snowshoe with Baldwin, for Chrissake. 'Fess up, Lou Quade."

"Nobody knows," answered the man called Quade. "Adams ain't saying and Zack Baldwin sure can't, and his son Ted only talks through a bottle."

"Wal, in any case, it ain't fair!" a fourth man, a townie, declared hotly. "If the line can't go through and has to bypass Forge, we'll all lose plenty of business. It ain't fair, one feller bein' able to halt progress that means a lot to everyone."

"No, it ain't," Latwick agreed vehemently. "Us citizens have a bounden duty to act, to take matters in hand."

Jessie glanced around at the angrily muttering men, and sensed the seething undercurrent that could explode into mob violence. "There's only one thing you people seem to forget," she called, hoping to reason with them. "Rufus Adams owns Moon Trail Canyon. You can't take it away from him by force."

"That's what you think!" Latwick snapped back. "I'm going to muster a meeting of businessmen and . . . Say, just who are you?"

"The name is Starbuck. And if you have a meeting, you'd better invite me, because I own Snowshoe Mines."

The men all swiveled and gaped at her, but their expressions quickly turned resentful and some nasty, low-keyed muttering began.

"Stop it!" Yates commanded hastily, glancing worriedly at Jessie. "Miss Starbuck is right. I appreciate your concern,

43

but my company can fight its own battles. It will, too—legally."

"What're you going to do?" Jake demanded loudly.

"Negotiate. Come to terms with Adams, even if it requires buying him out. All we're after is an equitable settlement on the right-of-way, and once he sees we're dealing fair and square, I'm sure he'll be willing to compromise. Now please break this up."

As Yates continued urging the group to disperse, the men gradually moved away in twos and threes, although they still kept muttering among themselves. After Latwick waddled back into his hotel, slamming the lobby door behind him, Yates sighed and took his pipe out of his jacket pocket.

"Thanks, Everett," Jessie said softly.

"It's nothing," he drawled, applying flame to fresh tobacco. "If you hadn't taken the first bite out of 'em, I was preparing to."

Smiling, she glanced from Yates to the hotel. "Sheriff Meek said this was the place to stay. Now I'm not so sure."

"Meek is right, and don't let Latwick bamboozle you. He's just a fat blowhard. If you want, I'll come in while you register."

"No, Ki and I have a few things to attend to first, and I know you're eager to see Roland," she replied, and stifled a small yawn. "We're fine. Nothing a good night's sleep won't cure."

"I feel likewise. Heaven knows, I won't get any sleep tomorrow night, on account of tomorrow being payday. Be trouble aplenty brewing here, and me trying to get my crewmen out of it."

"You'll have lots more trouble unless you can somehow strike a bargain with Adams. You sounded optimistic. Are you?"

"Jessie," Yates responded, compressing his lips, "I started

44

the PS&C with two short pieces of rusty track. I built it to what it is by gambling on long chances. I'm willing to keep on gambling, for high stakes. The road will go through."

Looking into his frosty blue eyes, Jessie had a feeling that, despite hell or Rufus Adams, the road would go through.

They parted, Yates heading up toward Doc Elgin's house. Despite their own needs, the welfare of their mounts came first with Jessie and Ki. They located a livery barn, paid the hostler two dollars for a single night's grooming and graining for the horses, then hunted up a restaurant.

An unpalatable meal of leathery steak and gumbo coffee, with sourdough biscuits extra, set them back another five dollars. In spite of the unsavory cooking and inflated boom-town prices, they ate greedily, and left the restaurant feeling immeasurably better.

They were starting back toward the Black Nugget, fig-uring on retiring, when abruptly a commotion arose some distance behind them. Pivoting around, they saw that down by the sheriff's office, men were yelling, a dog was barking, and people were turning and staring all along the street.

Ki shook his head. "Never a dull moment in Forge, is there?"

"Come on, we'd better find out what this ruckus is about," Jessie said, and they joined the crowd converging on the sheriff's office.

In front of the office door was parked a freightwagon, belonging, according to the scrollwork on its high sides, to Woodrow Fleishman. The driver was standing by the front wheels, gesturing excitedly while talking with Sheriff Meek. Spectators were milling about, peering constantly into the bed, shouting words that gradually evolved into a sort of chant:

"Rufus Adams is dead! Rufus Adams is dead!"

45

Chapter 4

The victim wasn't a pretty sight, for a shotgun had blown off most of his face, and another blast had made a crater of his abdomen. But his size, shape, and discernible features matched Rufus Adams's description—not that anyone cared to give the mangled corpse much of a scrutiny.

Jessie didn't care to give it even a peek. Ki examined the remains cursorily, and the only thing he thought odd was that Adams had changed his clothes. He was out of his lumberjack grubbies, and was wearing a plain, ready-made, and somewhat frayed black suit. In one respect it was more in keeping—it was a good burial suit, what was left of it.

Sheriff Meek was examining the cylinder of a Smith & Wesson .44 revolver. "Three shots fired, and recently," he noted, sniffing the chambers. He looked at the wagon driver again, who was a muscular chap with protruding eyeballs. "So you say that when you found Adams, this was lyin' in his hand?"

"No sir, the gun was beside his hand. When I came 'round the bend, there he was in the road, flat on his back and deader'n a mackerel, that gun there by his hand. And blood, gallons of blood."

"Nothing else, you're positive?"

"No horse, no sound or sight of anyone else. I couldn't very well leave him there, so I got out my tarp and brung him in."

"You did right, Floyd," Woody Fleishman said, having pushed through just in time to hear the last of the report. "Who is he?"

"Rufus Adams, Mr. Fleishman," Floyd replied. "You can take a gander at him, if you like raw meat. I found him about five, six miles nor'east of here, while I was deadheading back on the Moon Trail. 'Twas a gunfight, it appeared like to me."

Sheriff Meek nodded in confirmation. "Has the signs of one. There're his spent bullets, and all the blood; and from the way Adams's face and belly were shredded, there ain't no doubt the shotgunner fired upwards into him. He sure left us a mess to clean up, though." The sheriff gazed around. "Anybody know of any relations Adams had?"

A ragged chorus of noes answered his query.

"I don't either," the sheriff muttered, then brightened. "Here come the Paces. Well, that saves me a trip to Adams's camp."

Frantically, as if fearing to believe the news, the twins shouldered through and ogled the wagon. "Is he . . . ?" Ian faltered.

"Yep. Step close, boys, and pay your final respects. Then we'll cart him to Sneed's for burying, and that will be that."

"But ain't you gonna have an inquiry?" Olin demanded.

"Had one and closed it. Clear case of trading lead. Rufus Adams finally met a man who was faster'n he was."

47

"Shotgunned!" Ian choked, peering into the wagon bed. He turned, pale and scowling. "You're loco, Sheriff! That ain't no kind of gun duel, a shotgun against a pistol!"

Meek bristled. "Don't get sassy with me, boy. Adams shot three times, and you know as well as I do that he wasn't one to use a pistol if his target wasn't close enough to hit. And if you'd check how he was hit, you'd see that whoever did it must've been on the ground—anyway, below him. So there's a good chance, I reckon, that he wounded the other feller too. If he did, we'll soon know who it was, and he can tell us his side of the story."

"Which strikes me as plain sensible," Hilliard Latwick declared from the sidelines. "Don't try our patience, sonny."

Helplessly, Ian Pace glanced up at his brother, who had climbed up on the wagon seat and was leaning over into the bed. Then he glowered at the sheriff again, his body quivering with frustration. "Ain't you even gonna question Ted Baldwin?"

"What for? There ain't no evidence against Ted. In the second place, what evidence there is points to a fair fight. In the third place, Rufus Adams had a good killing coming to him. Hey! You up there, whichever Pace boy you are, get out and down!"

Olin Pace ignored the order. He was all the way in the bed now, hunkering close over the head of the body, his fingers maneuvering around the mouth. "Gawddamn! This ain't Adams!"

"Not Adams?" the sheriff blurted. "It has to be Adams!"

"He looks like him, but he ain't Adams," Olin stated. "This feller's wearing store-bought choppers. Adams has all his real teeth."

The revelation jarred everyone, even the imperturbable George Chaber. He moved forward, stepped on the hub of the rear wheel, and hoisted himself up so he could view the corpse better. "Sure enough. I can see pieces of an upper plate."

"Well, if he ain't Adams, who is he?" The sheriff waited. No takers. "C'mon, don't any of you know this man from before?"

"Yeah, from just a minute ago, when he was Adams."

The sheriff gave the heckler an exasperated frown. "I made an honest mistake, Sam. That body is mushed up something fierce."

"Why not search the man's clothing?" Jessie suggested. "He might be carrying a wallet or something else that'd help."

With patent distaste, the sheriff clambered, grunting, into the wagon. Olin Pace, grinning snidely, hopped off and left him to his squeamish search. It netted a meager handful of possessions, which Sheriff Meek displayed when he finally got down again.

"He sure traveled light," Meek remarked glumly. "A suspender button, a pocket knife, half a chaw of tobacco, and a buckskin money pouch with an envelope and a gold eagle. Ain't enough here to pay for burying him."

"May I?" Jessie said, taking the envelope and unfolding it. There was nothing inside, and the postmark was torn away with the canceled stamp, but there was enough left to show that it had been a letter addressed to Eugene Trevarro of Nogales, Arizona. She asked: "Does the name Eugene Trevarro mean anything to anyone?"

"Trevarro!" Latwick gasped. "Is that who's in the wagon?" He glanced around sheepishly as everybody eyed him. "I didn't recognize him. I mean, I didn't really look at him at all."

"Who's Trevarro?" the sheriff demanded.

"He checked in yesterday, him and his womenfolk," Latwick answered. "They're still at the hotel, I know. His

49

wife's Mexican and sicker'n a dog, and his daughter's been nursing her. The girl is cute as a bug's ear, and her name is . . . I remember, her name is Isabelle."

"You would remember that," the sheriff said sarcastically. "Well, go on, go get the gal to come see if this is her pa."

Smiling abashedly, Latwick hurried away. A few moments later he came bustling back, a young girl scurrying close beside him, her head bobbing along just at the shoulder of his jacket.

Petite, nubile, she couldn't have been more than twenty at the most. She had silky black hair over which she had thrown a light shawl, and a piquant face with ebony eyes, a snub nose, and a creamy, sun-golden complexion, which, like Ki's bronze coloring, denoted mixed heritage. She was wearing a colorful Indian-print dress with leg-o'-mutton sleeves and a belted skirt that accentuated the slimness of her waist.

Ki judged that the girl couldn't have weighed a hundred and ten pounds soaking wet. He also perceived, as she approached, that her features were drawn and strained, and that she moved with nervous anxiety. She stopped, uncertain, apprehensive.

"Howdy, miss," Sheriff Meek greeted her somberly. "I reckon Mr. Latwick has told you what we have to ask you to do."

"Where is my . . . my . . ." She swallowed, her eyes brimming with tears.

"Now, maybe he's not your pa anyhow. You just follow me over here, where you can peek 'tween the sideboards." Gently he guided the girl to the wagon. "Isabelle, is that your name? Well, Isabelle, take just one tiny peek, and it'll be all over."

Ki watched the girl's straight back, and observed how

her slender fingers gripped the boards as she pressed close to peer through the crack between them.

She stood looking without moving, as though she had turned into a statue. *"Papá,"* she whispered. *"Mi papá . . ."* Suddenly, without warning, her knees buckled and she began to collapse.

Ki sprang forward, but a man bumped rudely in front of him, ignoring him as if he didn't exist. It was Ted Baldwin, who caught her as she was falling, and she wilted into his arms.

Ki stepped back, smothering a grin, while Baldwin cradled Isabelle against his chest. He saw the young man's eyes widen as he gazed at the girl, down at her slender, tanned throat, where a pulse was barely perceptible. Ki noticed now, too, that her print dress was a bit threadbare, but clean and pressed.

The sheriff gnawed his mustache. "Shall I get Doc Elgin?"

"No," Jessie advised, "just some water will do."

"I've a little flask of whiskey," Latwick offered. "I use it to ward off mosquitoes."

The sheriff gave a snort. "There ain't a mosquito within fifty miles of Forge, Hilliard, and you know it."

The girl began stirring then, whimpering softly. Her eyes fluttered, moist and trembling. "Thank you," she murmured.

Baldwin helped her upright, his face flushing scarlet. He opened his mouth, but no words came out, merely a raspy gurgle.

"Miss Isabelle," Sheriff Meek said sympathetically, "if you feel able to, I'd like you to answer a few questions."

"My father," she moaned. "Yes, he's my father. Oh, my poor mother! This will kill her." She started weeping softly.

Baldwin cleared his throat. "There, there," he consoled,

51

finding his voice. He patted her awkwardly on the back.

"Miss, your pa was found on Moon Trail, some five miles from town. Do you know why he was going way out there?"

She looked blankly at the sheriff. "No, I'm sorry."

"Was he planning to meet someone, go someplace special?"

"I don't know. My father never confided in us."

The sheriff threw up his hands. Jessie, being familiar with the Latin custom of separating man's business from woman's work, thought perhaps a slightly different approach might gain more.

"Isabelle, when did you last see your father?"

"After dinner, about two hours ago."

"What did he say? What were you and your mother to do?"

"We weren't to worry. He might be gone overnight, and have a big surprise in the morning for us. Mother always worries, so he may've told her something more to calm her, but I don't know."

"Was your long trip from Nogales part of the surprise?"

"Yes, that's all he ever told us. Oh, and he wanted us to stay in the room, where it's safe. He said the town was bad, but I don't think it's half as bad as home. At least I didn't till now." Her tone was bitter, and she fought to contain fresh tears as she stared pleadingly at Jessie. "Why? Why was he killed?"

Sheriff Meek answered, hedging, "We ain't quite sure yet, Miss Isabelle." He gave her a brief account, leaving out his theory that the man had died in a gun duel, then he said, "Mayhaps robbery was a reason. Was your pa carrying money?"

"All we have," she replied faintly, "in his money belt."

"Any idea how much?"

"No, but we aren't very rich."

"Weren't no belt on him," the wagon driver hastily declared. "I brung him in like I ran 'cross him, I swear it."

"Calm down, Floyd, nobody's accusing you," the sheriff said. "Miss, your pa had only a ten-dollar piece, his gun, and some odds 'n' ends. You're welcome to take 'em whenever you want."

"My father wore a lizardskin money belt," Isabelle insisted. "Without it, we're . . . why, we're destitute."

"That's a terrible shame," Ted Baldwin said soulfully, "and we can't allow it. We gotta do something, gotta show you that Forge is a swell town, all in all. We'll take up a collection, that's what. And Latwick will let you stay in his hotel for free."

Latwick blinked. "I will?"

"No, no!" Isabelle exclaimed, drawing proudly erect. "It's very kind of you to offer, but we can't accept charity."

"Beats being broke," Chaber remarked, then ducked through the crowd and began sprinting toward his Black Nugget saloon.

The sheriff muttered under his breath, and refocused on the girl. "Now, it 'pears to me that your ma might know where that money belt is, or more 'bout what your dad was doin' and where he was goin'. Reckon it's worth me askin' her."

"Please don't!" Isabelle begged. "I'll ask her. Let me tell her about Papa, too. She's not very well, and the shock—" Tears welled again. "Oh, how on earth are we going to live?"

Baldwin patted her some more. "Don't give up hope."

The sheriff tugged at his mustache, pausing a moment before resuming his questions. Jessie interjected a few of her own, but they elicited no further information from the distraught girl. Then Ian Pace had a question for the sheriff:

"What're you going to do about your clear case of tradin' lead, eh? You plannin' to reopen your closed inquiry, now that it's her kin and not our boss who got a good killin'?"

Sheriff Meek sent Ian a baleful glance. "Danged if you ain't a pest, boy. The fact that the deceased ain't who we thought he was don't change the way he died."

"You're wrong," Baldwin stated flatly. "Isabelle's pop was a stranger and a family man. Him dyin' the way a rat like Adams would don't fit. Get investigatin', find a way that does."

"I'll do what I can," the sheriff retorted testily. "But you chew on this. Moon Trail was pretty dark when her pa must've been shot, darker than here in town. If I can confuse one man for another, so can somebody else. Somebody, f'rinstance, who's held a whiskey grudge against Adams, and has kept threatenin' to shoot him. Well, you want me to find a way that fits?"

George Chaber returned at that moment, bringing a woman with him. Most of the men thronging around knew the woman well, and greeted her warmly. Isabelle eyed her curiously. Jessie and Ki surveyed her with interest, particularly Ki, who, for a while now, had been discreetly studying the group, sizing each one up.

She was borderline thirty, plump-breasted and comfortably thighed, but far from being Rubenesque. Auburn hair, pinned in lavish swaths, framed a face that would have been termed perky in her youth, but was now shadowed by a certain hardness of eye, and a rather firm expression around her generous mouth.

Ki had already guessed she was Nanette Thrall by the time Chaber introduced her to Isabelle. He'd known too many women like her, typical daughters of frontier entertainment, not to recognize her style. On the whole, Ki enjoyed her sort. They didn't fool with that society-belle-virgin routine of coyness and teasing. When they liked you, they showed it, and when they didn't, they ended it.

Nanette immediately began running true to style. She maneuvered during the introduction to cut off Baldwin and clasp both of Isabelle's hands in her own. Her eyes flowed with compassion.

"George explained," she said, her voice a husky contralto.

The perplexed girl blinked. "He did?"

"Everything. Poor dear, I'm positively crushed to hear of your plight. You and your mother must move in with me at once."

Now Isabelle stiffened in protest. "You're sweet to suggest it, Mrs. Thrall, but we can't be beholden to charity."

"It's 'Miss,' and Nanette to you. George explained how you feel about charity, too, and this isn't charity. We'll work out something so you'll pay your own way. Can you sing? Or dance?"

"Why, I sing a little. And play the piano," Isabelle answered, slowly warming to Nanette's kindliness. "I don't under—"

"Nanette manages my dance floor," Chaber said.

"And the entertainment, and all the ladies," Nanette added emphatically. "I run a clean place, strictly on the up-and-up. And I can certainly use a good musician and singer."

Isabelle smiled slightly for the first time. "If I could work for you, Mother and I could stay here until we saved enough to get back home."

"Then it's settled. I won't consider any other arrangement."

Jessie wondered if perhaps Isabelle should consider some other line of work. Initially she had thought of objecting, but as she'd listened to Nanette Thrall and regarded her closely, she'd decided that the woman was sincere and her

55

dance hall was legitimate. Besides, Isabelle had shown herself to be a high-minded and resilient person, capable of recovering from life's cruel blows; and who better to help her tend her sick mother than a troupe of girls? After all, this was only a temporary solution.

Isabelle looked questioningly at Jessie, as if asking for another woman's opinion.

"Why not give it a whirl, Isabelle?" Jessie said, smiling encouragement. "What's there to lose? If it doesn't pan out, you can always leave, but I think you and your mother will be in fine hands."

Nanette Thrall tilted her head and surveyed Jessie with approval. "You're not so bad yourself, dear," she said in her throaty voice. "Drop in the Nugget, and have a drink on me. It's the only bar in Forge where it ain't a sin for a lady to enter. Not that such a sin, I wager, ever stopped you." She turned back to Isabelle. "Come with me, and we'll talk things over. There's only dead bodies here, and slack-jawed males—a wretched spot to bring a young girl. Oswald Meek, you oughta be ashamed."

"I am, but I didn't have much druthers," he retorted with a laugh. "Anyhow, the corpse is about to get moving, which is more'n I can promise for the rest o' these loafers."

Even as Nanette steered Isabelle away, the girl laid a hand on Baldwin's arm. "Thanks for being so considerate," she said, and gazed around at the others. "You've all been nice."

"Huh!" Nanette scoffed, dragging Isabelle away.

Ted Baldwin stared after her, dazed.

The sheriff began haggling with Fleishman over who was to pay for the state of the wagon and the hauling of Eugene Trevarro to the undertaker's. Some of the rubberneckers drifted off, satisfied they'd witnessed everything of importance. Jessie looked for Baldwin, impatient to get cracking on the Snowshoe Mines mess.

But Baldwin was impulsively heading after Isabelle, not rushing to catch up, but doggedly trailing, as if moonstruck.

Jessie called to him, but he never heard. "Damn," she muttered crossly to Ki. "Ah, well, let's head for the hotel. Maybe I can waylay Baldwin there. I'm going to bend his ear when I do. I've got plenty on my mind to say to that young buck."

Ki grinned wryly. "You can talk all you want to a deaf man, Jessie, but you can't ever make him listen."

Chapter 5

Considering the hullabaloo filtering in from the connecting saloon, the Black Nugget Hotel managed quite well to maintain an air of propriety. Inside was dim and cool, and would remain so during the sunniest heat wave, its windows shielded by heavy, full-length drapes. A rose-patterned carpet blanketed the lobby floor, a more subdued rose wallpaper covering the sides to the ceiling, and dark English oak serving as trim.

The reception clerk had an ax-blade nose perfect for sniffing haughtily, but he merely eyed Jessie and Ki indifferently when they checked into adjoining rooms. Jessie made arrangements for their small traveling bags to be fetched from the livery where they'd stabled their horses. Then she stood contemplatively for a long moment, not saying a word.

Finally: "Any plans, Ki?"

"Try the saloon, perhaps, see who's there."

"Good. I'll be in my room if you need me. We've come

up against some strange folks and happenings these last hours, and when my bag arrives, I want to catch up on my reading."

Her "reading," Ki knew, was a small black ledger that Jessie always carried on trips. It was a condensed copy of her father's notebook on the cartel, and was continually updated just like the original, which resided under lock and key at her ranch.

"Well, then, if I run into Ted Baldwin," Ki said deadpan, "I won't send him up to disturb you."

"You bring him up. I'll read him the riot act."

Jessie headed for the lobby stairs, while Ki strode toward the exit that led to the saloon. It was a wide archway, in which were set French doors. Ki opened the doors, stepped through, and immediately had to open doors in a matching archway. The narrow air space between the sets of doors, Ki supposed, functioned as a sound-deadener.

The Black Nugget proved to be larger than it had appeared from outside, and it was doing plenty of business. Thirsty drinkers were wedged three deep, keeping five bartenders busy at the ornate, mirror-blazing bar. Bounded by rows of occupied tables, the dance floor shimmered with Nanette Thrall's short-skirted girls, as they partnered townsmen and lumbermen, miners and railroad construction men, who in turn clapped hands and thumped boots in time to a fiddle trio.

There were a couple of roulette tables, a faro bank, several crap tables, and half a dozen poker tables. There were also tables for the convenience of hungry customers who favored laying a solid foundation before settling down to the serious business of drinking. A lunch counter catered to those who placed a higher value on time than on comfort. And over it all lay a pungent cloud of tobacco and lantern smoke.

Easing through the pack, Ki tried to spot familiar faces.

Ian and Olin Pace were at a table, celebrating the sheriff's foul-up. Isabelle and Nanette were not present, but that was to be expected. Latwick was absent, and so were Fleishman and his teamsters. Ted Baldwin was nowhere to be seen.

George Chaber was standing at the far end of the bar. He nodded cordially when Ki paused beside him and made a remark about Trevarro's peculiar death.

"More likely he was killed for his money than for any resemblance to Adams," Ki observed. "A lot of such robbing and raiding seems to be going on around here. It's hurting the railroad badly, and it's liable to hit the town hard, too."

"Makes little difference to me." Chaber smiled cynically. "People will always drink and gamble and make hogs of themselves."

"Haven't much faith in humanity, have you?"

"Not much. I've seen too much. I'm almost coming to believe that the only true honesty lies in men like Red Duvall, who pit themselves against the existing order and exploit the hell out of it. Duvall is honestly selfish, anyway."

Ki stared at Chaber, sensing derision in the depths of his eyes. Chaber, picking up his glass and giving Ki a mocking toast, tossed the drink back. Then, with a goodbye nod, the sardonic saloon owner went around the end of the bar and entered a back room, closing the door behind him.

"Chaber don't feel so sprightly today," a bartender confided to Ki. "He was real late back from ridin' yesterday, and was sore as a boil, with a hand burned to blisterin'."

Ki's eyes narrowed, while his tone grew genial. "Maybe he was saddlesore. Long rides can cause some nasty sadddlesores on folks who aren't used to riding regularly."

"Shucks, Chaber is in a saddle almost as much as he's in here. Sometimes he'll go for a day or two, and he don't necessarily tell us when to expect him. Keeps us on our toes, you bet."

Ki nodded thoughtfully and ordered a beer. The bartender drew it and moved away, and shortly the Pace twins waved as they left the saloon. Ki nursed his beer for quite a while after that, watching, constantly watching.

Eventually someone he knew entered. It was Sheriff Meek, who toured the interior with a practiced eye, then wandered over and let Ki spring for a beer. The same bartender served them, and the sheriff leaned to ask him, "Everything all right?"

"Fine so far, Sheriff."

"I got a guard posted at the bank, but I've a notion George Chaber's got more loot in his safe right now than there is in the bank vault. I'd twitch less if it all got moved over there."

"And I've got a notion it's safer here," the bartender retorted. "Chaber sticks at the end of the bar, or to his desk just inside the backroom door, and it'd make one helluva ruckus if anybody tried to get past Chaber and all of us."

The sheriff glanced at the door. "Where's Chaber now?"

"In the back room. You want I should get him?"

"Naw, no need, he knows the score. His cash here, his loss here." The sheriff swigged his beer and added grudgingly, "I plumb hope that for Chaber's sake it stays nice'n quiet here."

"The joint's been like a tomb tonight, I tell you."

"Looks wild enough to me," Ki remarked.

"You ain't seen nothin'," the bartender said. "Wait till tomorrow. It's payday at the railroad and a batch of other places, and it'll be whoop-and-boom from morn to closing."

The sheriff sighed. "No picnic for me, neither—"

The rest of the sheriff's lament was lost in an explosive roar. The eruption came from outside the saloon, and though a bit muffled by distance, it was a lamp-swaying, drink-sloshing, timber-quivering shock of a blast.

61

"What in Sam Hill!" the sheriff bawled, pounding for the door. Ki and most of the other patrons were close on his heels. Outside, they were immediately engulfed by people boiling from all directions, all yelling and gesticulating.

Pluming black smoke wreathed the bank building.

Shoving and bellowing, the sheriff plowed up the street. Ki ran alongside, helping him forge through the crush toward the two-story brick structure.

A moment more and they were before the bank entrance. Its heavy front door and barred windows were all blown out, and black-powder smoke percolated from their shattered frames. With the sheriff leading, they plunged through the entrance into the wreckage of the bank's customer area and main room.

They halted, the sheriff cursing between spasms of coughing as they peered around the pungent, murky gloom. Desks and cabinets were reduced to kindling, their contents scattered; and even the massive wood counter was toppled over, smashed, its iron-rod wickets bent and broken. On the far side of the room was the vault, its ponderous steel door lying on the floor, its dark interior gaping like an eyeless socket.

They made their way to the vault, already knowing what they'd find. "Nothing!" the sheriff raged, squinting into it. "It's been cleaned. But there weren't no reason to set powder to everything else! The bastards blew up the bank for the hell of it!"

"Or maybe to help them escape in the confusion," Ki said. He gripped the fuming sheriff by the shoulder. "The guard you said you'd posted here—where is he?"

Meek stopped swearing and stared at Ki. "I don't know. He'd ought to be here, leastwise pieces of him."

"Well, he's not. He's either sold you out and fled, or

62

he's around and maybe needs help. Or knows something that'll help."

"I'd trust Howard Egger with my life. I'm gonna find him."

They hastened back outside. The sheriff called to the milling crowd, asking if anyone had seen Egger, but nobody had.

"All right, then, I want some men for a posse," he yelled, and from the swarm of volunteers he quickly selected a dozen. "Ready your horses and meet at my office. The rest of you spread out and look for Egger, and I'll jug any idiot who goes in the bank!"

As the sheriff gave the mob a parting scowl, Ki suggested to him, "The rear of the bank should be checked, don't you think?"

Leading the way, Sheriff Meek trotted to the alley that flanked the left side of the building. He entered its pitch-dark maw and groped along a few feet, then stopped. "You'd best stay on the street. You ain't even armed."

Ki never paused, but moved on past the sheriff. "I'm sticking," he said firmly, gliding ahead, and the sheriff, muttering, had no choice but to dog right behind.

Ki stepped cautiously, his left thumb hooked in a vest pocket, his right hand clasping the short, curved *tanto* sword tucked in its scabbard behind his waistband. He scrutinized both sides and the path itself, remembering the rope-rigged trap in the Black Nugget alley. Nor had the sheriff forgotten.

But as they approached the building's rear corner, it was a window that first caught Ki's attention. "Look there," he said, pointing. "That window ahead. It's wide open, with the bars wrenched loose. Something's lying beneath it, too."

"You got good eyes. It's too dark for me to see nothin'."

Reaching the window, they found the object beneath it

63

to be the curled-up body of a man. The sheriff struck a match.

"It's Howard," he growled. He blew out the match and lifted the limp body in his arms. "Help me carry him to the light."

Ki picked up the man's legs, and started with the sheriff back to the street. There, by the dim glow of lamplight from surrounding windows, they made a swift examination. The man's face was pallid and blood-streaked, the blood having flowed from an ugly, coagulating gash just at the hairline above the right eye.

"Other than that, he appears to be whole. No bullet or stab wound or such," the sheriff said, relieved. "Still breathin', that's the main thing. What d'you figure got him?"

"I think he was hit with a gunbarrel," Ki replied. "He could have a concussion, but he's not done in yet."

Sheriff Meek turned to the bunch gathering around. "Some of you fellers take Howard to Doc Elgin's. And be careful how you sling him around. His skull might be busted."

Several men hoisted the unconscious guard, and gingerly carted him away in the direction of the doctor's house. "I hope Doc Elgin has plenty of beds," Ki remarked, staring at the departing figures. "At the rate he's been getting patients, he's going to be needing a full-size hospital."

"Hey, here comes Wilkes, the bank manager," someone shouted. A moment later a nervous, middle-aged man pressed his way to the front, mopping his brow with a linen handkerchief.

"Hello, Ralph," the sheriff greeted him, and quickly briefed the manager on the situation. "They didn't miss a dime, so far's I can tell. How much were you carrying in there tonight?"

"I won't know precisely until I've made a thorough accounting," Wilkes groaned. "Twelve thousand in payrolls,

I'd say, as a conservative figure. Oh my. Who could have done it?"

"The Red Devils," Sheriff Meek said. "Who the hell else?"

"Twelve thousand in small bills and coins, mostly sacked," Wilkes elaborated. "Quite a heavy load for horses to pack. Maybe you can run 'em down. Any notion where they'd head for?"

"For the Green River area," the sheriff declared, "in that big stretch of crags and timber just this side of Lester. That's where I lost 'em before. Ain't goin' to again, if I can help it. We'll give them Red Devils a good run, anyway."

Without further ado, the sheriff and Ki hurried to the livery for their horses. Very soon afterward, they and the other twelve men of the posse were galloping westward out of town.

Swiftly they rode along a winding wagon trail, toward the brutally wild uplands of which Sheriff Meek had spoken. Now and then the pale wash from a half moon would flow along with them, highlighting the trail's sharp twists and turns. But as often as not, churning, thick clouds would blanket the sky, darkly forecasting a storm.

The posse drummed on through the night, finally nearing the first steep slope of the area. Up this, through rugged cuts and breaks, wriggled the trail. A short distance to the north was the paralleling course of the railroad, and occasionally its shimmering steel tracks could be glimpsed. Just before the posse reached the slope, the sheriff called a halt and dismounted, and began inspecting a lengthy patch of soft ground.

"Yep, fresh prints of horses," he reported. "Weren't from freightwagon teams, either. It's them, all right."

Moving on, the posse climbed the slope and entered a gloomy gorge. This came to an end and the trail led along the lip of a precipice for a couple of miles, then dipped over a rise and descended sharply into a forested hollow. Midway across the hollow, a wooden bridge spanned a gully that was about twenty feet in depth by sixty in width. At the bottom of the gully surged a swift, shallow stream.

Onto this bridge thundered the posse, the hooves of their horses clattering on the worn planks. They were perhaps two-thirds of the way across when Ki felt the bridge sway under him.

"Quick!" he shouted, while heeling his roan to go faster. The posse was slow to respond, not sensing the impending danger, and Ki's horse was too tired, being a rental plug and not a great steed. Ki kicked again, yelling, "The bridge is going to fall!"

That it did, right then, in a convulsion. One splintering crash, and the bridge collapsed in pieces, hurling men and horses into the icy waters of the stream. Pandemonium ensued as the cursing riders strove to untangle themselves and get their frightened horses back onto their feet.

The water was not deep, but the walls of the gully were sheer. It was only after a fair mile of floundering downstream through the chilly mountain water that the bruised and battered possemen found a spot where the horses could climb the bank.

"The goddamn bastards must've sawed the bridge timbers most of the way through, after they crossed!" the shivering sheriff raged, wringing the water from his clothes and drooping mustache. "Of all the poisonous tricks! If we don't catch our death of cold, it'll be a wonder. But we ain't quittin'. Let's get going."

They retraced their way up the stream and began the ascent on the far bank, which consisted of soft clay. A suspicion, an intuition, started growing in Ki's mind, and by the time the posse was halfway up the grade, it had become too nettling a worry for him to ignore.

Reining in abruptly, he dismounted and scouted the ground. The rest of the posse slowed and returned, the sheriff chafing at the delay. After a few more minutes, Ki went over to him and said, "We've been outsmarted. They didn't come this way."

"The hell you say!" the sheriff barked, staring at the multitude of hoofmarks that scarred the trail's surface.

"I'm sure of it. If you look close, you'll see that all the prints are at least a day old. That is, except for one set of new ones, made by one horse."

Sheriff Meek swung down from his mount and studied the tracks. "You're right, damn it!" he concluded, his face mottling with anger. "Just one horse, headin' west, has passed this way since yesterday!"

"He'd be the one they sent on ahead to knock the props from under the bridge timbers," Ki said. "The rest of the outfit turned off somewhere."

"Well, let's go see if we can find out where," the sheriff said. "There's no sense in following that lone hombre."

Grumbling and cursing, the posse rode back downstream to a place where they could cross the gully. After regaining the trail they rode slowly eastward, surveying the frequently impenetrable sides for any sign of passage, and carefully investigating every opening, no matter how thin or shallow.

Finally, returning through the gorge, they arrived at the crest of the first slope. Ki pulled in and sat regarding the small, stony clearing around them, then descended from his saddle and once again investigated the trail's myriad imprints.

"This is the place," he announced, straightening. "All but that one man turned north."

Sheriff Meek and the possemen stared northward. The crest ended at a ridge, forming a vista from which could be seen a dark phalanx of fissured rock masses and towering forests, ringed by still higher mountain slopes.

"No followin' anybody in that dense patch," the sheriff despaired, throwing up his hands. "Not at night, anyhow."

The disconsolate posse continued eastward down the slope.

A mile beyond the spot where the sheriff had first found tracks was a low hill to the left of the trail. On top of this knoll perched a sturdily built, square house that looked like one block of solid stone. It had caught Ki's attention when the posse had raced past earlier. Then, of course, had not been the time to ask about it. Now Ki did.

"That's where Woody Fleishman lives," the sheriff answered. "He bought it when he started business here. Nobody local would, on account of its supposedly being haunted."

"Any reason to think so?"

"Naw, only some old-wives' superstition about suicides," the sheriff said. "Old Ezra Bass built it, nigh onto forty years ago, and hanged himself from a staple he drove in the beam over the front door. I've heard the staple's still there, but they took away the rope when they cut him down."

As they drew nearer, Ki gazed curiously at the sinister-looking house. Its massive oak door was shut, its unlighted windows staring blankly. Its ponderous walls gleamed coldly in the moonlight. Around the exterior grew scattered firs and pines, old and wind-blasted and peculiarly malformed.

Ki shook his head. "No, I don't believe in ghosts, but I don't imagine I'd care to pick that place to live in."

"Nobody else did either, until Fleishman. He bragged he wasn't scared of no haunts. Don't reckon he's scared of anything else, for that matter. Hard man, but I like him better'n George Chaber. I always get the feelin' that Chaber's laughin' at everybody, but I never seen anything about him that would make me laugh. Ain't either o' them the kind you laugh at."

Ki inwardly agreed, having found little so far that was humorous about the laconic freighter or the cynical saloon owner.

Shortly, the posse arrived back in Forge. Sheriff Meek shook his head in response to the questions bawled at them from the street, earnestly thanked his possemen when they pulled in by his office, and went to his quarters at the back to change his clothes. The possemen disbanded, mostly to various saloons.

Ki returned to the Black Nugget Hotel, collected his key from the sleepy clerk, and went up to his room. While he was unlatching his door, Jessie opened her door and peeked out.

"Ah, it's you," she said. "How was the chase?"

"No luck."

"Too bad. I've had a little better luck. Want to hear?" She locked the door after Ki entered her room, and stood with arms folded across the bosom of her calico wrapper and Empire-style nainsook nightgown. "I was bathing when the blast hit, so I missed most of the action. When I heard what had happened, though, I went to Dr. Elgin's and offered to nurse the guard."

"To *pump* the guard, you mean."

"Didn't have to. Couldn't shut Egger up, after he came to, although he can't recall a thing after going to check a noise in the alley. He'll recover fine, but the doctor gives Superintendent Roland only a fifty-fifty chance. Anyway, who should come visit the guard but the banker, Wilkes, and naturally that led to us talking. Ki, his bank was looted of nearly twenty thousand dollars."

"It's worse than he first thought," Ki said, frowning. "Did Wilkes say if his bank can stand such a hefty loss?"

"It's the shareholders who have to make it good. They're all shopkeepers and landowners and so forth, the kind you find around every small town—plain, solid citizens who don't have money to waste, but are willing to buy stock in their community. But in this case, Ki, there's an extra angle. Most of the bank's shareholders are also investors in the PS&C. By standing the losses, they're draining capital that Yates needs badly."

"Interesting. Is George Chaber a stockholder?"

"One of them, but not the largest. Wilkes said the biggest stockholder was Fleishman. Why?"

"Chaber refused to deposit his saloon's proceeds today," Ki replied. "Maybe that's his habit. I don't know, but it seems odd for a bank owner not to be his own customer. What about Rufus Adams, Jessie? Does he have stock?"

"No. So it's no loss to him, only gain."

"Sure, robbing the bank helps stop the railroad. I catch your drift, Jessie. You believe the robbers were aware of this, that they were out to get at it, as well as at the bank loot."

"I'm convinced they were." She shifted to the window, and peered distractedly through the curtains. "But if they've got two targets, why not three? Break the bank and crush the railroad, and they've ruined the investors. This area's financial and commercial backbone would collapse, triggering such a depression that the entire region could be bought for pennies on the dollar."

Ki was doubtful. "Jessie, aren't you giving a backwoods bandit gang too much motive? The Red Devils couldn't handle so costly and complicated a scheme, and besides, why would they or anyone else want to try? There's nothing that valuable here, is there?"

"Not that I'm aware of—yet." Jessie turned, smiling mirthlessly. "But the Devils are capable enough, or rather, those backing them are. I did my homework tonight, Ki. I boned up on my reading. There's no mention of anyone we've met so far, but I did find an old reference to Red Duvall. Short but sweet."

Ki's eyes narrowed. "The cartel?"

"He was in it, at the time. Duvall ran gangs on the Seattle and Portland docks, smuggling, shanghaiing, white-slave trafficking. He tried extorting protection money from the Starbuck import business, which was how he ended up listed by Alex. That's all, really, except for one curious fact. Duvall earned his moniker 'Red' from having once been lynched. He was hanging when friends saved him, and the noose left a hellish rope burn."

"That's a switch! Everybody's hunting a redhead."

"Duvall might be one anyway. The reference doesn't give a description of him. Still, it adds something more to go on."

Ki went over to stand by Jessie at the window. He glanced out, seeing a farm wagon rattle down the street, and hearing a fiddle scrape in the adjoining saloon. Then, inclining his head, he regarded Jessie with a weary yet affectionate expression.

"Miss Starbuck, it adds a barrel of snakes, that's what."

Chapter 6

Early as it was when Jessie arose, the main street was already
packed with men. She was baffled, until she recalled that
today was payday.

Dressing, she went next door. Ki answered her knock,
and they left the hotel in search of breakfast, becoming
instantly swallowed in the jostling swarm. Most were railroad construction workers, with more yet rolling in on flatcars. But miners and lumberjacks, arriving on mules and
horses or stuffed in company wagons, were also cramming
the street, boasting of their plans for the money that was,
or soon would be, in their hands.

Jessie had experienced similar payday celebrations in
other small, remote towns. The idea was for all employers
within drinking range of a town to pay on the same day,
so they'd merely have to contend with one big blowout,
rather than numerous smaller toots. Often it worked, raising
output and reducing hangovers, and proved popular with

72

most crews, who liked partying together. Inevitably, though, there'd be some bosses who'd refuse to agree. Knowing this, Jessie doubted that every single camp, company, or operation that might conceivably pay wages and be within riding distance of Forge was here this morning. It only felt that way.

Many outfits still paid off wages in hard coin, but she noticed that plenty of others had chosen to deposit their payrolls and issue checks. It was hard *not* to notice; the bank was mobbed with check-waving workers. Incredibly, the bank was open, Wilkes and two tellers sitting at tables before the gutted entrance. They couldn't cash checks, of course, but appeared to be trading them for little paper chits—the bank's IOUs, Jessie surmised. Probably Wilkes had been up half the night, having some printer make them, and he'd likely spent the other half of last night convincing the local businessmen that his chits were the same as cash.

After an awful breakfast, Jessie and Ki walked to the railroad depot, where the crowd was thickest. Faces craned southwesterly, where the tracks curved into the hills on their circuitous descent to Tacoma.

Jessie felt tempted to go see if Everett Yates was home in his coach. Since their parting, she'd recalled him now and then—not dwelling or daydreaming, but with spontaneous and vivid impressions of a gesture or a glance or some similarly fleeting detail that had appealed to her. That was what it boiled down to, she had to admit; the man appealed to her, so naturally she wished to be in his company.

No, the pleasantries had to wait, she told herself sternly; Everett would be too busy with payday, and she had her own work to do. Her temptation thus having been quashed, Jessie turned and surveyed the gathering, just as she'd been scanning around her all morning.

"Not a trace," she said to Ki. "Do you see any sign?"

73

Ki shrugged expressively. It was too teeming and bois-terous a crowd to allow accurate spotting of one man.

Suddenly a shout went up, and swelled to a roar. At the pass of those southwestern hills, a shadow-blurred black object had appeared, crowned by a dark and wavering plume.

"Here comes our dough!" a brawny tracklayer bellowed. "Line up, boys!"

Swiftly the black object grew and took shape, slanting rays from a cloud-hampered morning sun glancing off its diamond stack and elongated cowcatcher. A humming vi-brated the rails, increasing to a staccato crackling, then to the pulsing rumble of driving wheels. A spurt of steam soared over the boiler of the locomotive, a 4-4-0 Cooke, whose simple wheel arrangement allowed it to negotiate the sharpest curves.

Seconds later the eerie wail of a whistle reached the crowd. It was answered by whoops and hurrahs. The pound-ing engine unit and its "bobtail" haul of modified baggage car and a "shorty" caboose came trundling and swaying over the poorly ballasted track. A switchman twirled a lever, and a white marker flashed red. There was a sudden cutting-off of the hammering exhaust, a trailing cloud of smoke that shot upward again as the roar of the blower quivered the air.

The pony trucks of the locomotive took the switchpoints. With a clanging of brake rigging, a screeching from the rising safety valve, and a banging of couplers, the train ground to a halt on the sidetrack closest to the depot.

Armed guards descended from the caboose and took up posts along both sides of the baggage car. The pay doors opened, the brass-grilled windows banged up. A steady stream of men began filing in one door and out the other. Payday was in full swing.

Around the car and depot, impatiently waiting construction crewmen pressed forward, squeezing, arguing, hassling for position. Having no reason to stay in such chaotic bedlam, Jessie and Ki fought clear, leaving the trainyard and heading back up the main street.

"It's crowded here," Ki remarked, "but it's better."

"No, it's not. I don't see Ted Baldwin anywhere," Jessica stated, her voice peppery. "Maybe he's hiding from us."

"Jessie, I think maybe he's not in town."

"He should be here. Isabelle and the payday are, and how could he leave them? Ah, perhaps Isabelle gave him the gate—"

"Or Nanette gave him her boot," Ki interrupted dryly. "As for payday, Jessie, Baldwin can holiday any day, which evidently he does. And you're only assuming the Snowshoe is included in this shindig. You don't know for certain, do you?"

"How could I?" she flared. "Baldwin's not around to ask, and and the records are back in Texas. Sure, weeks ago at the Circle Star, I'd have checked if I'd known this payday existed! I still could, by telegraphing the ranch." She paused, let out a long breath, and said calmly, "All that, when it's not worth checking, much less bickering about. Sorry, Ki. Well, if Baldwin's not here, where?"

"I'd guess the Snowshoe Mines, where he's supposed to be."

"Now, that'd be novel . . ."

They hastened to the corral of the livery stable, and got the hostler. Fifteen minutes later they were leaving Forge.

Guided by the hostler's instructions, they readily located the fork for Moon Trail. They loped northeastward along its sinuously twisting, rutted surface, with a partially overcast sky developing above, and stony outcroppings and tall-wooded flanks encroaching on all sides.

Occasionally they would spot work trains rolling toward

Forge, loaded with men. The PS&C's rail-end was much farther ahead, someplace between wherever they were and Moon Trail Canyon.

They admired the infrequent views of ribboned steel while snaking among the cliffs and valleys on the old outlaw trail—a trail whose main idea, unlike that of the tracks, was to gouge the worst possible route through the meanest terrain available.

They pushed on well into midmorning. The sky continued to be unstable, either broiling in clear sunlight or chilled under gray, drifting clouds. It happened to be sunny when they entered a pocket canyon through which the trail looped in a kinky S-curve. Its sides were so low that it could hardly be defined as a canyon, and its dished bottom was small even by pocket standards. It was overgrown with tall grass, scrub, and thickets of aspen, fir, and pine, all pressing right up along the shoulders of the trail, hindering sight of anyone coming or going.

Midway through, and shielded by both curves, the roadbed showed a big blotch, as though something dark had spilled and soaked in there, leaving a residue. There were plenty of animal and wagon tracks to and fro through it, but they hadn't deterred the insects from swarming on its surface.

Jessie reined in. "This must be where Trevarro's body was found. I want to look at this, a good look."

Dismounting, they staked their horses with cinches loose and graze underhoof, then methodically went to work quartering the area. Both could track and read sign, for Jessie had grown up with Ki teaching her techniques that he'd learned from his samurai master, Hirata. Since then, they'd improved their abilities in one of the best schools in the world, the American Southwest. Skilled as she was, Jessie would still give the nod to Ki, for he had a naturally keen eye and wide peripheral vision that no amount of training could match.

Now, in silence, they studied the ground, not making any comparisons until they had both read all the sign visible to them. Then, while Jessie circled slowly around, Ki went to the dried pool of blood. Here he stood, gradually turning around while his dark eyes searched every inch of the gritty road within eyesight. When satisfied, he waited quietly for Jessie to finish her search. Finally she came over.

"All right, Jessie," he said, "tell me what you read."

She nodded gravely. In a way it was a game, one they had played many times before, but they both took it seriously, because it was serious education. Life-and-death serious.

"There's the mark where Trevarro was riding north," she began. "He was shot and fell where the blood is, and there's a sliding mark indicating one foot slipped under him. Over to the left, in that thicket, a man was hiding with a shotgun. I didn't find any spent shells or wadding, but I did make out where he walked out to stand over Trevarro, maybe to be sure he was dead."

"Uh-huh. What kind of shoes was he wearing?"

"Size nine or so blucher, with that odd sole. Well, up ahead the teamster stopped, got down, and came to look. There are scuffmarks from Floyd's tarp, probably, and more where he lugged the body to his wagon. That's it, Ki. Trevarro was shotgunned off his horse, and don't ask me to fill in the details. I can't."

"I can't either, Jessie, not by sign alone. We'll have to guess at it." Ki pursed his lips, contemplating, then said, "We know Trevarro dropped. A shotgunner couldn't have done it, not from that range, not without hitting the horse. So the man in the brush stood up and fired a rifle."

"Ki, there's only one shotgun buttprint over there!"

Ki nodded calmly. "In this weather, in this soil, the average shotgun and rifle would leave the same crumbly indentation."

"That's not it. Where'd the shotgun come from?"

"From a second man. There'd have to be two, one to ambush Trevarro, while a second distracted him while riding by. Assuming this, the second man carried a *very* sawed-off shotgun. A brushgun. Why?"

"Easy. You can hook a brushgun under your coat. Otherwise, Trevarro would've spurred faster. He came from Nogales; he wouldn't palaver on a dark, isolated trail with a man holding a long-barrel."

"All right. Trevarro is down. He's dead or so close to it that the rifleman feels safe to come up. He or the other man swipes Trevarro's pistol, fires three shots, and drops it. Then the rifleman trades for the shotgun, and triggers both barrels point-blank."

"That's it!" Jessie gasped. "Sheriff Meek got it backwards. Trevarro was on the ground; the killer was over him, not under him. But it'd look the same, look like the shotgun's buck ripped upwards." Jessie's excitement ebbed as, thoughtfully, she reviewed the sequence of events. "Ki...I've another idea."

"Good. Shoot."

"Don't say that! Well, the second man hides his shotgun—not necessarily a sawed-off one—in, say, the nearby grass. Then he plays injured or sick. Trevarro sees a plainly unarmed man in great pain, and reins in. The rifleman doesn't stand up, but fires through the bushes."

"Yes. Yes, I see your logic. We don't know of any local reason to kill Trevarro, a stranger. We do know he resembled Adams closely enough to fool people. We know Adams's reputation is such that a hired gunman would take extra care to keep back and low. An unarmed decoy, he could take risks his partner couldn't. Anyway, it strengthens the theory that Trevarro was killed by mistake."

"Some mistake! One man dead, two women shorn of

husband, father, and all their money. The word will spread as word always does. The killers will find out. Or maybe they did find out when they looked at Trevarro, and shotgunned him out of spite."

"Listen!" Ki cut in urgently. "Something's coming."

Jessie stiffened, concentrating, then heard the odd sound. At first it was an angry rumble, as of storm winds blowing southwest from the canyon, then it quickly swelled to a deep, rhythmic pounding, a ground-drumming roll, highlighted by sporadic snapping noises.

"Plenty's coming," Jessie said, and glanced swiftly around. "Come on, let's move where we can see them before they see us."

They grabbed their horses by their bridles and plunged into the trail-hedging grass. Nearby sprawled a vaguely circular clump of boulders, and diving through a crevice, Jessie and Ki found a tiny, grassy patch well sheltered by rocks, though still very close to the trail.

Hurriedly they ground-hitched their horses, which were becoming increasingly skittish, pawing and snorting from the approaching tumult. At quickening speed it was sharpening into the thunder of horse hooves, the wrench of saddles, the hoarse profanities of whooping men. Even the occasional snappings were now recognizable as the spasmodic firing of handguns.

They focused on the far sweep of the S-curve, just as the first push of riders careened around the bend. Behind them streamed more, a looming flow of big men on big horses, wearing work clothes and low-heeled boots, their features black-etched from ground-in coal grit.

Ki smiled. Miners! A mining crew on payday!

Jessie did not smile. She stared in awe at the sight of this human tidal wave bearing down on them. Well, it wasn't really a tidal wave, or even that large a crew; but it didn't need to be, squeezed as it was within the pocket. The men were driving toward Forge at a headlong clip, yelling and laughing, shooting capriciously, jousting one another and vying to be a horse-nose ahead. Among the forty-odd men galloped one miner noticeably younger and thinner, but no less rowdier, than the others.

"Baldwin!" Jessie cried. "That's *my* miner!"

"They're *all* yours," Ki called back, his smile cracking wider. "There's Lou Quade, too, so this must be the Snow-shoe crew."

The Moon Trail blurred under their horses, and as they came abreast of the boulders, a couple of the miners tried some fast-paced target practice. Jessie and Ki hugged their stone cover, hearing potshots ricocheting off rock. Suddenly Jessie's roan bucked, squealing, stung on the rump by a rock shard. Breaking hitch, it bolted through the boulders opposite, followed by Ki's equally spooked horse. They disappeared into the woods beyond.

Cursing, Ki gave chase. Jessie dashed after him, while the oblivious miners swept on around the next curve to disappear, much more noisily, in the other direction.

Searching for their horses didn't take them long or far. Like most livery rentals, the roans were docile and disinclined to wander freely on their own, and were shortly found grazing placidly in an open patch next to the woods. After checking them and the gear and tightening cinch straps, Jessie and Ki mounted and returned to the trail.

"There's hardly much need to go on," she said testily, watching the dust plume that marked the miners' route. "Most of what I wanted to see is going back to town. Shall we, too?"

"All right, but at our pace, not theirs." Ki eyed the exasperation stamped on her face, and sighed dolefully.

"Poor Ted Baldwin. He doesn't know it, but he's in for trouble."

"Don't worry, Ki. He'll know it before I'm through."

The intermittent morning sun was shrouded by noon clouds when Jessie and Ki arrived back in Forge. It didn't seem to be sorely missed; the town was enlivened quite well without it. The main street was a turbulent swamp, easily absorbing Baldwin and crew, and overflowing into shops and eateries. But the most jammed and raucous places were the long-barred saloons, where gaming tables thrived, and whiskey poured unceasingly. Fiddles and guitars resounded, boots clumped on dance floors, and voices crescendoed, interspersed by shouts and bawlings of what was supposed to be song.

"What a stew," Jessie said as they neared the livery. "The only ones not here must be the Red Devils and Adams's crew."

"Of the two, hope for the Devils," Ki suggested. "I'll bet Adams has timbermen like Baldwin has miners, and if both outfits got drunk here together, they'd take the town apart." Ki rubbed his ear thoughtfully. "I wasn't so curious before, Jessie, but now I'm wanting to know just how badly Adams deserves killing. And by whom, other than Baldwin. Or maybe Baldwin is the killer."

"I'm not about to overlook Baldwin," Jessie promised.

"Well, while you're not overlooking him here, Jessie, you won't be needing me. I'd like to go look at where our posse got thrown last night, to scout around some before the light worsens."

"Fine. I'll meet you whenever."

They parted, moving to do what each felt was necessary, making no complicated plans that might go awry, but using

81

events as they occurred to shape future actions. So, while Jessie angled toward the livery, Ki headed out of town.

He was damned glad to be out of it awhile, Ki thought as he loped southwest along the wagon road. He could enjoy such crowded conditions for only a short time, and after that his tolerance took a nose dive. Out here he could be at peace, admiring the unspoiled vistas as he rode, and enjoying the warming sun when it won a battle with the clouds. Yet his empathy with nature also made Ki hope that the clouds would prevail and bring a drenching. The timberlands were summer-dry, becoming hazardous without rain.

He passed the rise upon which stood Woody Fleishman's house, and it seemed to Ki that it looked even more austere than before. For a moment he pondered what singular disposition of the freighter could prompt him to reside amid such bleak history and surroundings. When no answer came readily, Ki dropped the question and rode on, leaving the gaunt abode gleaming coldly in high daylight.

Reaching the clearing at the crest of the first slope, he reined in by its north edge, where the bank robbers had descended. He hooked a leg comfortably over his saddle-horn, and studied where their prints slewed down loose shale to hard stone, and vanished into a tall forest's shadowy undergrowth. Then he surveyed the looming hills, trying to figure where logically the robbers might have left the forest.

Finally he gathered the reins and, after some coaxing, took his horse down the shale to the forest. Tracking from there proved as difficult as he'd feared. The earth was partly clay, hard from lack of water, but mostly volcanic crumblings that shifted, impressionless, under pressure. It was layered by conifer needles, also useless; and above that was mainly dimness, up to the bottom tree branches, which were higher than Ki on horseback.

Scraped tree bark, hoof-clipped rocks, and trampled vegetation led Ki slowly through the forest. If he'd read their path right, he realized, they'd exited far from where he'd figured they should have. And it didn't get any easier for him after that, either.

A half-dozen times, Ki had to rein in to carefully study the broken stone ledges and thicketed breaks that stretched from the forest behind him. Twice he found he'd strayed off course and had to backtrack, tempering his impatience. And once he got lost and wound up in a box canyon, then overshot his return, passing the point where he should have resumed his tracking. When he realized this and swung back, he came upon the path.

He noticed it by chance, and could easily have missed it, the path being no more than a single-file ribbon where passing hooves had beaten the ground raw. And yet, all things considered, Ki judged he would eventually have traced the robbers to the path; and since it was meandering more or less in the same direction he'd been tracking, he decided to try it for a while.

Turning onto it, Ki jiggered his roan into a trot. The path wound through stony gulches, flinty hogbacks, and thick but spotty groves of brush and timber. He maintained a steady pace until suddenly the path veered to the right, toward a gorge. The gorge was steeply sloped, hopper-shaped, heavily overgrown with pine and scrub, with a fairly wide stream curving out from the mouth of the floor. Far and long on both sides ran a wall of rock.

The path grew rougher, like a washboard, and narrower, with encroaching vines and briars. Between him and the stream, and some distance to his left, were a number of groves with similar undergrowth choking the spaces among the trees. As he continued along toward the stream, it became apparent to Ki that its water was not irrigating the land, for he saw too many withered plants, brittle bushes, and thorn patches that were losing their needles and stickers.

He was just passing the first of the groves when he felt a hot sting crease the nape of his neck. The echoing crack of a rifle sounded an instant later, followed by a wisp of gunsmoke rising from the grove.

Ducking, Ki kicked his horse ahead. The rifle fired a second time, followed by four or five riders galloping his way. He hunched lower across the saddle, the thorns and nettles raking his skin and clothes as he goaded the horse on. The rifles kept up their fusillade, and now, dimly, Ki could also hear the yelling of men and the rataplan of pursuing hooves.

Mean trouble, he figured, but he'd been in worse places. He had a good head start, and at their distance, targeting him from horseback amounted to sheer guesswork. As long as he could maintain his lead and not get bagged by a lucky shot, he should be able to dodge and lose them somewhere soon in this rough terrain.

Then, suddenly, a bullet whined by from another direction. Twisting in his saddle, Ki saw four more men galloping down at him from a grove diagonally ahead to his left. With them in front, his escape was blocked, while the first bunch in back cut off any retreat. If he angled due left, they'd converge tangentially on him, and rapidly be within easy shooting range. And to turn right would confront him with that stone wall, the long, steep base of a slope with no visible access for climbing.

Now, Ki admitted ruefully, he was in a worse place.

Chapter 7

Frantically searching for a way out, Ki decided his only chance—if you could call it that—was the gorge. Its mouth, from which the stream flowed, was a few hundred yards ahead and less than half a mile to his right, not impossible if his horse held up. It was starting to blow hard, a sure sign of weakening; but it was also beginning to panic from the gunfire, as it had before.

If Ki had worn a pistol, he'd have triggered it beside the roan's ear. Since he hadn't, the best he could do was kick its ribs and flail the reins, while yelling like a banshee.

With everything that was left in it, the livery rental responded. Slugging its head above the bit, its eyes rolling, its nostrils flaring, the horse lengthened its body over the ground. Now that Ki was fleeing at an angle to both groups, though, they were rapidly able to close the intervening gap. Ki could hear the crack of gaining rifles, and sense the bullets whipping by, many of them dangerously close. Yet every slug sizzling by or kicking up spurts of dirt and rock only added to his horse's hysteria. Terrified, it fairly boogered across the final yardage, hurtling into the mouth of the gorge even while Ki was feeling the wind of passing lead.

Once within the narrow slot, Ki breathed easier. It was choked with similar briar and brush thickets to those outside, and despite the stream, much of the growth was equally dry—indicative, Ki thought, of the floor and streambed being of hard stone, and of the topsoil being a shallow cap. Yet conditions were fertile enough for most plants to grow thick and chest-high, giving him the advantage of cover. His pursuers would pay a heavy price if they tried to find and finish him amid this tangle. And with darkness just a few hours off, he could hole up safely here till nightfall, when escape would be an easy matter.

For some distance he let his horse run headlong through the brush, ignoring the lashing branches and scratching creepers. Once he was well concealed and its fright had been exhausted, he gently slowed the roan's pace to a trembling walk. "Calm, calm," he kept repeating soothingly. "We're doing fine now."

When the roan began acting as if it might halfway believe him, Ki turned to listening intently while he rode. But as he drove deeper into the gorge, the only sounds that broke the silence were those of the burbling stream, or those of small animals aroused by his own passage. Gradually, however, another noise started to intrude. At first it was a whisper that grew to a murmur, then to a subdued splashing.

It could only be a waterfall, where the stream flowed over from above. Since it seemed to be emanating from straight ahead, and the sides showed no indication of making a bend, Ki reasoned that the fall was on an end wall. And that meant the gorge was a box.

Well, being in a box cut some of his options, but Ki felt it didn't change his basic choice. Either his pursuers left him alone and he laid low till dark, or they tried to smoke him out, and he killed them till dark.

Then, abruptly, an acrid smell stung his nostrils. Sniffing sharply, feeling his eyes begin to smart, Ki realized that to smoke him out was exactly what those men had in mind. They'd set fire to the dry brush in the gorge, and a breeze was blowing it toward him. They had him literally backed to a wall.

Sensing the danger, his roan quickened of its own volition, plunging forward as fast as the dense growth would allow. But stronger and stronger grew the tangy reek of wood and stewing sap. Blue wreaths and swirls began fouling the clean air and dimming the bright sunlight, and, borne by the wind, there rose an ominous moan that grew and deepened to a droning roar.

Ki coughed from the fumes. His horse snorted, head tossing, body shuddering from inhaling lungfuls of smoke. The brush became thick almost to the point of being impenetrable, so Ki veered his horse to the stream and waded into the water. It was shallow, fortunately, and the floundering horse managed to stumble over its boulder-strewn bed.

The air was so heavy now that breathing was growing painful. Hot ash and burning brands, whirled aloft by the fire-created vortex, were showering down and threatening to ignite fresh blazes ahead of them. Rushing up from behind, flames were sweeping through the gorge in a crackling, roaring wall of fire. Ki's face was set hard, almost brutally, and his eyes were cold as he listened to that rapidly advancing inferno. He was scared—anybody sane would be scared of burning alive—but he was stoic about dying, and enraged at the men who'd torched the timber, and was convinced that to avoid the former and get at the latter, he must not panic.

Other than that, he was fresh out of ideas. Meanwhile he kept prodding his frenzied horse, compelling it to plow up the stream as fast as possible. Gradually the surge of the waterfall drowned out even the wailing of the fire. He was closing on it, though it was yet hidden by the intervening brush and the winding of the stream. He pushed on, coaxing his horse forward.

Rounding the bend in the stream, Ki glanced over at the fire. A vast column of smoke was boiling skyward, and beneath it licked hungry tongues of flame. The air was stiflingly hot, noxious with smoke and acrid fumes. Ahead he could see growing flickers where falling embers had kindled the dry growth. Then, finally, he saw the fall, perhaps a hundred feet from the rear lip of the gorge, plunging amid clouds of spray into a catch-basin at its base. From there poured the stream, flowing gentle and serene.

But the fall itself was not so placid, and as Ki stared with smoke-reddened eyes at the spewing torrent, he began to wonder. Then to hope. He veered his horse to the left bank of the stream, and urged it to scramble up to a little rocky strip that bordered the water. Straight for the back cliff he went, and under the shelter of its overhang he dismounted and gripped the horse's bit. Then he stepped toward the surging fall.

The horse balked, a great deal of white showing in its eyes. Ki pleaded gently, then spoke more firmly, and finally, his senses reeling from the fierce heat of the fire, he argued loudly with the horse. The horse ogled the enveloping spray, and refused.

The fire was scant yards away, leaving him no choice. Ki plunged into the falling water, shouldering against the cliff and dragging his horse after him by one prodigious effort.

The horse resisted, but its steel shoes kept slipping on the wet, bare stone. Still, between its prancing and the water's force, Ki was almost knocked off his feet a number of times. But before he lost his balance altogether, the hope he'd felt turned out to be true. Close to the cliff face, the falling water was only a thin sheet of the overflow, mostly mist and spray; and between the body of the fall and the cliff face was a shallow space.

There was scarcely enough room for Ki and his horse to hug the damp face of the cliff. In front of them surged the fall, a misty green curtain that slowly began glowing with fretted fires and opalescent tints, and other vivid hues which Ki knew were the result of firelight being filtered through the flow of water. The air, similarly filtered by the fall, was clean and breathable. They were the only things to appreciate, so Ki appreciated them.

The horse was miserable, shivering and snuffling.

Gradually the kaleidoscopic waterfall resumed its normal translucence, indicating that the fire was burning itself out. Ki waited a while longer, discussing trust and cooperation, only to wind up dragging the horse back through the water.

The gorge was still cloaked in smoke, but, pushed by the prevailing breeze, the murk was slowly dissipating. Remounting his horse, Ki rode slowly downstream through the hot and fuming air, seeing scattered patches of growth smoldering and glowing, but no indication of the main blaze, which had died for lack of fuel. Finally he reached the mouth of the gorge, and wasn't surprised when he found no sign of the men who'd set the fire. Doubtless they'd ridden off, confident that he'd been consumed and reduced to nothing but charred bones lost in the blackened gorge.

After scanning the terrain in the waning rays of sunset, Ki rode eastward. As much as he'd like to, he couldn't hope to pick up the track of those men in the deepening gloom. Moreover he was chilled, famished, and exhausted; and the prospect of the long return to Forge was completely unappealing. The way back could be shortened, he figured, by not going south through the forest to the crest, and then northeast down the slope. Instead, by heading straight for the wagon trail, he'd intercept it much closer to town, and cut out that lengthy dogleg.

So, purposely, Ki blazed a fresh path on what he hoped was a direct route to the wagon trail. He rode the stone ledges and rough brakes of the unfamiliar country, full night having long since descended when at last he came within sighting distance of the wagon trail. Heartened, he patted his horse encouragingly, but the most it could muster was a weary slog in that direction.

Then, rounding a blind hillock, Ki glimpsed a glow to his right just ahead. At first he thought it a peculiarly low and lurid star, but nearing, he recognized it as a lamplit window atop a knoll. Drawing abreast, he finally discerned the rigid bulk of the building, a hard black against the softer black of night. It was the haunted house of Woody Fleishman.

Ki swung his horse sharply up the knoll. It wasn't impulsiveness or gnawing curiosity, but practical necessity that detoured him. He felt numb from exposure and hunger, but he had merely to ride. His horse was shambling, threatening to collapse, and might not make the house, never mind Forge. A light in a window meant somebody was home, and far as Ki was concerned, the code of frontier hospitality forbade even ghosts from turning away any cold and tired and starving stranger who came knocking.

Dismounting before the inset front door, Ki started up two broad stone steps, only to hesitate midway as he heard strains of music drifting from within. It was the unmistakable plucked throbbing of a full-sized harp, but the melody was unfamiliar to Ki—not that he was ever a great connoisseur of harp compositions.

As Ki started up again, a dog suddenly barked inside, and the playing ceased. Low, growling snarls followed him to the door, but the instant he knocked, they stopped too. Then there was utter silence.

After a long moment, Ki was about to knock again when the lock snicked back and the door swung open on oiled hinges. The old man who stood gazing out was extremely tall and thin, of a type that one ranch foreman Ki knew liked to call "a snake on stilts." But that wasn't what perked Ki up, any more than were the man's ordinary work shirt and pants, or his totally bald head. No, it was his sad hound-dog chops and benevolent brown eyes and mild demeanor. He seemed totally harmless, but every instinct in Ki warned that he was not.

"Yes?" The man had a voice made for confessionals.

"If you can spare it, food and rest for me and my horse."

The man thought, and appeared ready to think a lot longer, when a woman's voice called from within: "Bring him here, Jericho."

The old man stepped aside, ushering Ki in and closing the door. Ki stepped into a large, dark-paneled room that was comfortably, even richly furnished. What caught his eye immediately was a gold-leafed concert harp that reared on its pedestal between two wide windows. At the harp was seated a young woman of provocative beauty, who regarded Ki with yawning indifference.

Ki doffed his hat, nodding politely. "Good evening, ma'am."

She ignored him, other than to continue staring with pale blue eyes that were lidded, luminous, and bored. Her face was soft-angled; her hair was brassy and hung in an abundant bob; and her lips were burgundy and, save for her single yawn, expressionless. From what Ki could perceive under her too-small, candy-stripe percale wrapper, her figure was far from indifferent.

The man said, "Now, Valerie, we can't invite guests."

"He invited himself," she replied, her voice cool and flat. "Besides, he's here now. Go put something on to cook, Jericho."

Old Jericho clucked his tongue while leaving the room, but his rebuke left Valerie unconcerned. Ki placed her age at about twenty-five. He found her disinterested study of him a bit goading, like an offhand challenge.

"I've got a horse to tend to," Ki began, taking a step toward her. A mistake. From behind an overstuffed chair at the far corner lunged a growling, fang-baring brute of a dog.

"Dog!" Valerie snapped, and the dog halted protectively between her and Ki. "Don't touch him, mister. He'll chew you."

Ki shrugged amiably and leaned forward. "Hello, Dog."

The dog went berserk, barking and slashing, on the verge of pouncing. But Ki noted how carefully he stayed where Valerie had positioned him, and after a few minutes he quieted down to low hostile growlings.

"Mister, if he gets you, he's got you."

Ki squatted and stretched out his hand, palm up, and the dog went crazy for a while again. Ki tried again, and kept trying, talking soothingly, his gaze steady on the dog's smoldering eyes while the animal raged and snapped suspiciously.

He was getting a rise out of Valerie too, Ki saw. She was smiling strictly for him, very faintly, with a twist of mockery. But about this time her dog's responses were growing more uncertain. His lips curled, then lowered, and Ki, chuckling, leaned nearer. The answering growl became almost a querulous whine.

When Ki noted the dog's tense muscles starting to relax, he reached forward and scratched under his lower jaw. He continued shagging the hairy coat upward and behind the ears. Then he paused, and the dog, who'd been motionless till now, butted his muzzle into Ki's palm and began snuffling with a damp, chilly nose.

"I don't believe what I'm seeing," Valerie gasped, amazed.

"He's about half-wolf, isn't he? But a dog's a dog," Ki said as he rose. "Now about my horse—"

"Our stable's in back," she cut in eagerly, thawing now that the ice had cracked. "There's a lantern in the kitchen. Oh, and there's a washup next to the tackroom, if you've a mind."

Thanking her, Ki exited through the same door Jericho had taken, and was drawn by a clatter of pots and pans along a hallway. Entering the kitchen, he found the old man puttering about a cast-iron stove, but he had to look longer to find the lantern on a peg.

"Sorry, no scraps, son, and your meal'll be a while yet."

"Sure," Ki replied heartily, matching Jericho's beaming refusal. "I just want the lantern. I'll be a while, too."

After lighting the lantern, Ki went out the rear door. He saw the dark barn of the stable about a hundred yards distant and just a little below the hilltop. The beauty of its location dawned on Ki while he stepped around front for his horse. Either by chance or by design, the stable was set where it was invisible from the wagon road.

Walking his horse to the stable, he stripped and stalled it, and filled the stall crib with sacked oats. Then, as the horse drowsily munched, Ki borrowed a few more supplies to give it a quick curry and rub. He didn't want the roan to get sick now, not after it had tried so hard, and might be called on to try again.

He angled for the tackroom, in the front of the stable by the saddle racks, thinking of what he'd found other than livery supplies in the stable. Not much. No farm gear, but this wasn't a farm, and no freight gear, but maybe Fleishman didn't bring home his work. No horses, Ki's roan having the pick of stalls and corrals. Just sizable supply stocks, plus a great many tracks, a dirty clutter in the stalls, and the truly imposing manure pile out back, all indications that numbers of horses were stabled here upon occasion.

Beside the tackroom door was a bench upon which rested a basin, soap, and a water bucket. Above the bench, on the wall, were a cracked mirror and a dirty roller towel. Ki took the bucket to the trough pump, but, reconsidering, put the bucket aside, stripped bare-chested, and sluiced noisily in the horse trough.

Rising, he pivoted in the direction of the roller towel, while whipping his head to spray some of the water out of his hair and eyes—and stumbled, arms outflung, into Valerie.

She gasped, startled, and fell against his chest. Mashed between them was a long, fluffy bath towel, and when Valerie looked up at Ki, taking her time about moving from his wet embrace, she said lamely, "I remembered about that old roller, and thought . . ."

"Why, thanks." Smiling, Ki began toweling his bare chest. "I'm sorry, I wasn't watching. I'll get dressed as soon as I dry off."

"Oh, not on my account. I've seen men," she said, then faltered as if embarrassed. "That came out wrong, didn't it?"

"No, fine," he assured her, retrieving his shirt and vest, and he started toward the stable. "We'll go, as soon as I check my horse a last time."

Walking beside him, Valerie said, "Then you'd best give me these," and she deftly took the towel and his vest and shirt from him.

94

Nodding thanks, Ki left her in an open area between the tackroom and a low mound of nearly fresh hay. He went along the stalls to his horse, and began looking for late swellings or bruises, while from the front of the barn, Valerie carried on a conversation.

"Mister, are you happy?"

"I think so. Why shouldn't I be?"

"Most of the time, I wish I were."

Having checked his horse, Ki headed forward. "Well, why aren't you?" he asked her, and could have kicked himself, for he wanted to stay cautious and a bit distant.

He found it suspicious that no one had yet asked his name or offered theirs—which was all right in itself, since all he wanted to do was eat and get some sleep, and not become involved in any business that had nothing to do with him. Still, it was a bit strange.

He didn't see Valerie right away. Approaching the open area at the front of the barn, Ki failed to glimpse her even when he held his lantern aloft.

"Valerie? Where're my clothes? I want to go eat."

"Don't go. Change your mind," she answered, so close to Ki that he almost tripped over her. She was in the hay, the towel spread beneath her, lying on her side and leaning on her elbow. She blinked, smiling, in the lanternlight. "I changed my mind."

Ki sensed a bad shift to the wind. "What do you mean?"

"Don't sound so dreadful, mister, it's all normal and natural." Valerie was twisting gracefully as she spoke, easing up into a low, predatory crouch. "I go a long while, it's like I'm dead inside, and my mind says give up, what's the use..." The girl was now stretching as a tiger would, and Ki could swear she was breathing that heavy feline way, which in cats produces purrs but in Valerie produced husky passion. "Then, you see, something *happens!*"

Ki set the lantern down and held his chest high. "Oh no," he muttered to himself.

"You happened, mister," she continued. "You came here with your dog tricks, and shocked me something fierce." She rose from the hay to stand before him. "I can feel. I'm alive!"

That, Ki considered, was a great understatement. Her percale wrapper had been laundry-boiled over the years to the opacity of gauze, and draped almost translucently over large, pointed breasts. The lanternlight was bright enough to show him the sharp points of her nipples pushing against the fabric. The position of the lantern on the floor also focused the beam between her thighs, and the way she stood, proudly hip-shot, it was brazenly apparent that she wore nothing else beneath the wrapper.

He simply wasn't up to this, Ki told himself. Yet, in spite of his resolve, his eyes measured her breasts' impressive roundness and the shadowed delta of her svelte loins . . . and he groaned softly, thinking her wrapper might as well be a *yukata*, that short, thin body sheet which acts as a boudoir kimono . . .

Valerie pulled Ki down to the towel. "Isn't this nice here?" she remarked chattily, then stared in Ki's eyes. "It's gospel, all it takes is a jolt when I'm that way. Like your astonishing me. That's how I get this way. Well, one of the ways."

Valerie lay back on the towel and her breasts pushed, unfettered, against her thin percale wrapper. "'I wonder how come such a pretty li'l thing is such a roundheels,' right? Isn't that what you're thinking?"

"No, I was thinking you don't even know my name."

"Huh! I don't want to know it. And you know more of my name than I want. And I bet you wonder about why I do it, I bet. I do, I know. Loving a man, wanting babies and a nice home..." She grinned and tugged at Ki. "Lie back. I know why I do it."

Ki turned and grabbed her instead. "I know too, but can't it wait?" he pleaded, as they scuffled in the hay. Valerie ended it, sitting up and scrunching around close to Ki, but at a slight angle, so she could pick the hay out of his hair.

She said, "Later?" Ki nodded and said, "I promise." She laughed and drew her legs higher. "It can't be later. You'll be gone tomorrow. I'll be gone from you. Now or never."

The close angle allowed Ki to catch glimpses up her wrapper, its hem having twisted up over her knees. When Valerie saw what Ki was doing, she moved her legs apart a little so he could see better.

Valerie eyed the beginning bulge in his crotch, and with mock primness she moved her hem down and sidled next to Ki. "Y'see, it's emotion. That's why I do it. When you feel it strong, you have to run with it. Catch it like when a fellow is hard, and work it."

They sat side by side, Ki with his legs bent slightly, and Valerie with her legs thrust out in front of her. She smiled at him and moved her hand to take his, pressing his fingers into the giving softness of her breast. She flexed her hand atop his, digging his fingers into her warmth. Ki pressed, tweaking her nipple. She took a breath, shuddered, and moved his hand down to her leg.

Ki ran his hand up her leg. She put her legs together, and after a bit of rummaging, he pulled them apart.

"That's my resistance. I never give up without a struggle," she said, and squeezed his arm. "You like?" she whispered.

"I like," Ki admitted.

"There's more," she said.

Ki parted her thighs and slid his hand between them, his fingers teasing the soft undersides. Then he pulled her wrap-

97

per up all the way to her waist. Valerie put her legs out straighter and looked at them. Then she turned her face and kissed Ki, her lips parted and wet. She breathed in, moaning with pleasure, and her very eagerness fired Ki on. With both hands deep in soft flesh, he extended his tongue tentatively, carefully. She accepted it, sending shivers of delight through him as his hot probe went deep into her mouth.

Valerie held him tightly to her with jerks of her arms, and his mouth meshed with hers. "If we took our clothes off and did it right here," she whispered, making big, wet sweeps of her lips across his mouth, "do you suppose someone would come?"

"Let's try it and find out," Ki said.

Valerie sat up and began unbelting, unbuckling, and undoing tiny eyehooks galore. Ki dealt more quickly and surely with his own rope belt, and had his jeans and slippers off very quickly.

He lay back nude, all the while thinking he was a damn fool for allowing this. But what the hell, a stiff prick knows no conscience, or sense of decency or danger, either.

Finally she disentangled herself from her wrapper. He let his eyes feast on the gleaming alabaster of her body. She held her breasts in her hands. They were large enough so she could cup their undersides and push the taut nipples out as she leaned over him and rubbed her breasts against his chest.

Easing closer over him, she parted her lips and tasted his mouth again. This time she offered her tongue, moaning with the sheer heaven of it. She pushed him slowly back until he was lying prone. Then, moving down, she closed her mouth over his erection.

She seemed to be trying to take all of him. The hot, smooth, thrilling closure of sucking warmth forced Ki to squirm with growing passion.

Valerie put her hands under his hips and encouraged his movements, giving with his upward thrusts, taking as much as she could. She brought her tongue into play, touching his tip ever so lightly, then darting back as if too shy to continue. Then, clamping her mouth over him as tightly as she could without causing pain, Valerie commenced a pumping action that drew little gasps out of him.

"It's now," he panted, "or never!"

She laughed, low, liquid. She lay full length on him, pushing his hardness toward her warm, soft depths, clinging to him, reaching between them for his rigid shaft so she could guide it into her loins. In return, Ki lunged upward in sheer lust. She moaned in her eagerness and pushed her hips and thighs downward to take him, deep and hot and sliding, far up inside her pulsating belly.

Ki gripped her shoulders, his fingers digging in as Valerie gasped with pleasure. Her firm, rounded buttocks rose from his loins in a smooth, sinuous arch, then pressed down, down, and drove his spearing manhood wetly into her. Her inner thighs and delta were greedy and slippery for more to fill her eager cavern. The fulfilling length of Ki's erection was given up reluctantly, until all but the head was exposed for an instant, then it was reclaimed until her flaxen-haired delta was pressed tight against his curly hair.

Valerie moaned with every long, downward thrust of her hips. Ki was in the throes of his imminent release, and his hands locked spasmodically around her tautly undulating buttocks, pulling her down with urgent power, grinding her tight, forcing every bit of himself into her.

She shivered and then convulsed. But Ki was so lost in his own orgasm that it took a moment before he realized that she, too, was pounding, jerking inner muscles in tempo with his pulsing ejections. Soft walls held deep muscles that moved in spasms of delight, enclosing him tightly, throbbing ecstatically. She spread her legs wide, pushed down, and held the last bits of joy there between her legs.

"You like?" she laughed softly.

"I like," Ki said, gasping for breath.

"There's no more," she told him. "No more." Slowly, sighing contentedly, she eased herself off Ki's limp body and retrieved her wrapper. "Your shirt and vest are over on the bench."

Ki just lay there as though vanquished.

"I won't be eating with you. We won't see each other, except mayhaps a brief spell tomorrow morning." She paused. "Please don't tell. Forget it happened."

"Not a word. I won't forget it, but I won't tell." Ki rose and began dressing. "Fleishman will never hear of this from me."

Valerie paused, her eyes wide. "Wh-what?"

"Woody Fleishman. He lives here, doesn't he?"

"I guess you know he does, or you wouldn't be here," she answered bitterly. "And here I thought you were—"

"Needing help tonight?" Ki offered, when she didn't finish her thought. "Well, I was. Look, I don't know any more than that he lives here. I was told that much when I rode past yesterday."

The look he got in response was clearly etched with suspicion, if not downright disbelief. Valerie shrugged her shoulders, finished shaping the drape of her wrapper, and left the stable without so much as a goodbye nod.

Ki went over to the bench, where he finished his washing and dressing. He went to the rear door, knocked, and was ushered in by Jericho. "Well, about time. It's getting cold, son!"

By the finish of the meal, Ki decided that whatever else Jericho was or was not, he was a ferociously bad chef. He told the old man that, and was rewarded with a jubilant smile.

100

Valerie was not in the living room, nor was her dog. So Ki had to ask Jericho where he was to bunk. The old man told him, and Ki climbed the steps and found the room, the first one on the left. The bed was comfortable, and he was soon asleep.

Sometime during the night, Ki awoke. He lay for a moment trying to decipher the noises, and figured out they were horses outside, followed by murmuring downstairs someplace.

He continued listening, and eventually heard someone ascending the stairs. The person was not treading furtively, but with that purposeful tread of one who knows exactly where he is heading.

The steps passed his room and kept on down the passage. A door creaked open, then closed. Silence followed. As it remained unbroken, Ki turned over and went back to sleep.

★

Chapter 8

After Ki left her, Jessie stabled her horse and searched for Ted Baldwin, with no better luck than she'd had that morning. Looking was harder, the congestion thicker and drunker than ever. Miners, timbermen, and other laborers were spending fast enough to avoid having their money burn holes in their pants. But they were pikers compared to the railroad workers, who outnumbered them by five to one, and squandered their wages at about the same rate.

The street helped as best it could. Shopkeepers, booze-merchants, and trollops hawked their wares, eager eyes promising what rarely was delivered. Waxen-faced dealers sowed and reaped a chip harvest, while shirtsleeved bartenders chain-poured glasses, and saloon chippies cadged drinks with too-ready smiles on their too-red lips. And then there was a sprinkling of men who appeared to be workers but who, Jessie knew, were anything but.

These were the men who, at one point, caused Sheriff Meek to detour from his rounds and join Jessie. "If those sons don't pull somethin' by dawn, I'll eat my badge. Hill vultures seekin' carcasses to pick—and ready to make 'em, if need be."

"Speaking of carcasses, have you seen Ted Baldwin?"

"Earlier, him and some miners was down by the depot. Baldwin, a carcass, that's a good'n! S'long." Chuckling, the sheriff tugged his mustache and returned to his rounds, veering off to investigate the innards of a canvas tent dead-fall.

Jessie walked toward the bottom of the main street, scouting both sides to no avail, but seeing a freight train steam in from the direction of rail-end. As she headed for the depot, she watched its approach, hearing the exhaust swell and deepen, the low rumble become a grinding roar.

Abruptly the exhaust was closed and the couplers clanked together as the train quickly lost speed, nearing the new roundhouse. The switch to a siding flashed red, the engineer slackened speed still more, and the slowing locomotive nosed onto the chosen track, in the shadow of the roundhouse wall. Jessie could make out the engineer leaning out of the cab, one hand on the brake handle. The fireman stood in the gangway between engine and tender, gazing out at the town.

Suddenly, with no warning, a cloud of gray-black smoke gushed from under the locomotive. There was a deafening roar, a rending of metal, and a rumble of cascading bricks. Through the turmoil knifed a scream of agony, cut short.

Through the billowing smoke cloud, Jessie, stunned by the shock of the explosion, saw the locomotive actually rise in the air. It careened off the tracks and turned over, then disintegrated with a thundering roar as its boiler exploded. Huge chunks of steel sailed through the air. A nearby outhouse was demolished by a section of hurtling boiler. More bricks flew wildly from the shattered roundhouse. Jetting steam clouds streaked through the smoke, and for a long instant all details of the disaster were blotted out.

Swiftly, though, the smoke and steam dissipated. Where the tracks had been a moment before was now a wide, deep crater, with wisps of smoke rising from it. One entire side of the roundhouse had been torn away. The roof sagged crazily on its splintered beams. The turntable had been blown from its pivot and lay, smashed and twisted, in the pit. Of the fireman and engineer she could find no sign.

The depot and trainyard were a turmoil of near panic. From behind, crowds were boiling from the saloons and eateries, shouting, gesturing, thronging in and milling around the scene, to stare awed at the crater, bawl angry questions, and curse for lack of answers.

Everett Yates, his eyes like burning cobalt, sprinted from his coach and shouldered his way to the front. A score of paces distant from the track, he spotted a portion of the mangled engineer. The fireman was apparently nothing but scattered fragments. Parts of the locomotive were strewn in every direction, along with splintered crossties and twisted rails.

Sheriff Meek came burrowing through the crowd. Glimpsing him, Yates began striding to meet the sheriff that much sooner, then saw Jessie and angled closer to her as well.

The sheriff intersected him first. "Sounded like a bomb," he declared irately. "Black-powder bomb, I'd bet on it. Some skunk planted it under the tracks and set it off when the train came."

"God, that's hard to believe!" Yates protested, although with his own eyes he was forced to believe. "The track is patrolled, and we have our own security. Only way would be if one of our own construction workers was a double-crosser. But I trust them all!"

"Wal, there's the evidence," the sheriff said grimly, making a sweeping gesture while glancing around. Catching sight of Jessie nearby, he called, "Miss Starbuck, did you get to the depot? Did anything explode before the boiler blew?"

Nodding, Jessie came up and said to Yates, "Afraid so, Everett. A charge went off under the engine, just like a bomb."

"Believe me, I'll find out how it got there," he vowed grimly. Then, with a light pressure of fingers on Jessie's arm, he turned her so he could speak confidentially, out of earshot of the sheriff and others. "This is presumptuous of me, being short notice and all, but I think we should get together to talk soon."

"Of course, anytime."

"For dinner, in my coach at seven-thirty?"

"Fine."

"My pleasure. Until then, unfortunately, I'll have this to contend with." Yates turned back, saying in a louder voice, "Thank God, Sheriff, this isn't worse. If this had been one of our trains loaded with workers this morning, instead of a freight..."

The sheriff and Yates began ramrodding the sometimes grisly tasks that needed to be done. What could be found of the dead fireman and engineer had to be located and carried away, and the rubble had to be searched for any more victims. A gang was dispatched to repair the tracks, its crewmen handling their tools gingerly, as if fearing that other bombs might be planted about.

The tragedy cast a pall on the payday spree. As the crowd dispersed from the trainyard, some regrouped tensely in the street, while others headed back home to their jobs. Most went to the larger, more conversational saloons such as the Black Nugget, to discuss over drinks this latest outrage.

The Black Nugget was where Jessie went, to eat, rest, and not cause a scandal—if Nanette's word was true. The saloon was comfortably full when she entered, with small groups quietly drinking or playing desultory games of poker. George Chaber was at the end of the bar; Nanette stood talking to some dancing girls, and three musicians on a rear dais were playing mostly ballads.

Nanette flashed a smile and bustled over. "Glad to see you," she greeted Jessie warmly. "I know Isabelle will be thrilled, too. She's going to play piano in a few minutes."

"What can I do to help her, Nanette?"

"You're kind to offer, but we've done about all. Her and her mom are moving in with me tomorrow, and she'll have a decent time of it here, I'll see to that. I've got to dash. See you later!"

Watching Nanette leave, Jessie marveled at the painted dance-hall mistress playing a proper nanny to a pair of refined ladies. It was more than generous; it was incongruous.

But genuine, she thought as she walked into the saloon; and too precious to be mocked at by a saloon owner. She eyed Chaber, who smiled pleasantly enough, but it seemed to Jessie that there was a quirk of sardonic amusement on his classically handsome face.

Seated only a few paces distant was Woody Fleishman. He didn't smile, but gave Jessie a speculative glance and said, "Good evening, Miss Starbuck. Please join me for a drink."

"Not right now, thank you. I'm looking for Ted Baldwin."

"Sorry." He leaned forward. "I've a proposition, though."

Resisting a laugh, she sat down. "I'll pass on the drink."

"At least you joined me." He clasped his hands on the table, and fixed his eyes on Jessie. "We each know who the other is, so I won't spar. The railroad will go through, in spite of Rufus Adams and a few others, and it will clobber my business. Possibly kill it. If it does, I'll go down swinging. It wouldn't be the first time I've been down and had to start over."

"Is that why you came from Calexico, to start over?"

"From that area, yes. You do your homework, I see. I'm doing some too, to find something else to get into. The bar trade, maybe. Chaber's making a mint. Or a mining outfit, if it's not very big or in very good shape. Like the Snowshoe, to be blunt. At the right terms, I might propose to buy the mines from you."

"I might accept. First I want to look the mines over, which I'll do as soon as I let my manager know I'm here."

"Baldwin not knowing sure sounds familiar." Fleishman straightened to take out his pocket watch, and Jessie, glancing past him, spotted Isabelle wending her way toward them. Then, repocketing his watch, Fleishman said, "You stay put, Miss Starbuck, and sooner or later Baldwin will be in. He has his reasons."

Jessie nodded. "One's coming now."

Fleishman twisted his head to take a quick peek at the girl, then turned his gaze back to Jessie. "A pity. Chaber really should spring to send her home. She's not the type to mix here."

"Who is the type, Mr. Fleishman?" Jessie countered, in a tone that implied he'd somehow insulted her. Before he could respond, she looked past him again to Isabelle, who was just now approaching their table, and called to the girl cheerily in Spanish.

Clapping her hands, Isabelle replied delightedly in kind. She gave Fleishman a sweet-eye, and added a little flounce of her off-the-shoulder peasant blouse and pleated skirt. Her only effect was to make Fleishman cast a questioning eye at Jessie.

"I believe she wants you to dance," Jessie confided.

"You're right, f'sure," Fleishman agreed, and said ruefully, *"No, gracias, no, Señorita."* He rose to his feet. "I'm overdue now, way behind time. I'm sure you understand, Miss Starbuck. Goodbye, I'm sure we'll meet soon. *Adios, Señorita."*

Fleishman headed briskly for the entrance. Isabelle looked to Jessie and gave a quizzical shrug. Jessie didn't respond at once, her attention having been attracted to a nearby table.

The group of husky men there were suddenly leaving, abandoning half-filled drinks and smoldering cigars in a rush to catch up with Fleishman. They were garbed in corduroys and high-laced boots, and for the most part had the brawn of timbermen or miners or other outdoor workers. But their features also had a hard-eyed, sullen wariness that Jessie thought was more the result of a locked-up existence than of carefree outdoor living.

The musicians ended their final tune, and left on a short break. Isabelle looked at the upright piano on the dais, then at Jessie. "I'm to play now," she said, half-urgently, half-crossly. "Tell me, why'd you say I wanted to dance with him?"

"A joke." Jessie chuckled devilishly. "Oh, oh, his face!"

"And me showing off my clothes, like you asked." Isabelle caught the infectious humor and began giggling. "He bounded off like a rabbit! It's terribly funny!"

"Don't tell, we'd get in trouble," Jessie warned, and Isabelle promised with a conspiratorial nod as she hurried toward the dais. Jessie stopped smiling, and sat thinking while she watched the girl play. Tinkling strains of the untuned piano came lilting through the saloon, as Isabelle confirmed her dual heritage in the cowboy and *vaquero* tunes she chose. Jessie continued listening, contemplating, her eyes frequently searching the room.

Then, on one of her sweeps of the saloon, her eyes

108

narrowed slightly at the sight of the man who'd just entered in company with four miners. Boisterous Ted Baldwin, tipsy but not soused, of willful expression and petulant lip. She had him, Jessie thought; now it was simply a matter of where the moth would alight.

His miner companions split off to dance or gamble, while Baldwin strutted to the bar and struck up a conversation with Chaber. Jessie couldn't hear it, but judging by Baldwin's mugging, it couldn't be very serious. She rose, figuring to interrupt.

Baldwin swaggered over to Nanette then, to banter with her. Jessie had started closing in on him, when Isabelle started to play "The Cowboy's Lament." The sentimental ballad was one of Jessie's favorites, and apparently one of Baldwin's too. The opening bars stopped him talking, the first verse turned him around, and the rest lured him to the dais as if pulled by a rope.

As Baldwin climbed the dais, Jessie was more than halfway there, and Isabelle's sweet voice was lifted in the sad song:

"We beat the drum slowly, and shook our spurs lowly
And bitterly wept, as we bore him along . . ."

The steps to the dais platform began about a yard from the rear doorway, and they ended up facing the piano, which sat across the platform at a diagonal. So when Jessie passed the closed door on her way to the steps, she could look up and see that Isabelle was truly grieving while singing. Baldwin was draped on the piano, believing right along with her, all calf-eyes and melancholia.

Just as Jessie topped the steps of the platform, Isabelle's hands made a discord and her voice broke, choking: "For we all love our . . . our . . ." She bowed her head against the music rest and began sobbing uncontrollably.

Jessie sprang to the piano, bending over Isabelle with a comforting arm and consoling words. Baldwin hovered fretfully, aware that he'd be holding Isabelle if he'd been an instant quicker, but otherwise aware of nothing else that could be done. There was nothing, Jessie knew, having learned from her own father's death and from those affecting others, that anguish couldn't be calmed but must be purged. Isabelle wept copiously, the best remedy for draining sorrow from one's system.

Suddenly, Jessie grew aware of noises behind her. The shuffling feet, a rusty hingepin, gasps from near the dais, a startled warning cry from Nanette... all so swift, short, and muddled together that she sensed more than heard them. Alarmed, Jessie began reacting, stiffening, turning—

"Lady!" Baldwin was shouting. "You!"

Pivoting in a high crouch, Jessie glimpsed a split-second series of actions: three men bunched in the open rear door, unrecognizable in the shadows, their faces covered by bandannas and their hats tugged low. A few body portions were visible in the saloon's lantern glow, such as feet or a beer gut, or the two right hands holding revolvers, or the third right arm snapping forward in a dexterous motion, its hand holding a knife by the tip.

"Look out!"

Jessie, still swiveling, with her right hand drawing her custom pistol, had her first flashing image of Ted Baldwin. His mouth was open, yelling at her, and terror was in his eyes, and panic was sending him scrambling, snatching the first thing that came to hand. A gleam of light intruded, sparking from the knife blade as it sailed from the thrower's fingers in an unerring trajectory toward Jessie or, if she moved, Isabelle.

Baldwin came out of her peripheral vision, lunging forward and swinging a violin belonging to one of the musi-

110

cians, thrusting it before Jessie like a shield between her and the flying knife. With a jarring, splintering thud, the blade stabbed into the violin, stopping its course mere inches from its victim.

The knifer and one gunman started fleeing away from the saloon's rear door. The third man was backing, swiveling to follow, aiming his revolver for a parting shot, to salvage their thwarted murder. Jessie was still circling, her Colt swinging level in her grip. Baldwin was lowering the knifed violin, gawping as if he couldn't believe he'd done such a feat.

The gunman fired. His shot angled low, striking the side of the dais, a bullet from Jessie's pistol having already struck him, entering about at his breastbone and exiting about kidney level. Except for a general weakening of limbs, which resulted in his gunbarrel drooping when he triggered, the man seemed paralyzed from the impact of the lead, mouth wide as if to scream, but no sound emerging.

Jessie was in motion, even as her bullet struck. She paused to glance at the shattered violin and captured knife, which Baldwin was still holding wonderingly in his hands.

"Thanks," Jessie said. "That's one I owe you."

Then she jumped from the dais and plunged for the rear door. Baldwin, dropping the violin, was taking the steps from the dais, calling after her, "Lady! Lady, it ain't safe!" Coming to the doorway, Jessie leaped at the gunman, snatching his pistol from his nerveless fingers and throwing it back into the saloon, then diving out into the field behind the saloon.

"Don't do that!" Baldwin cried irately, the pistol having narrowly missed him. Hesitating a little as he approached the door, he ogled the gunman she'd shot. The man's legs buckled and he toppled over, and Baldwin leaped over him as though over a fallen log.

"You'll get kilt, lady!" he yelled. He ran up the alley,

111

crying, "Come back here, afore you get kilt!"

"I'm right here," Jessie said calmly, standing at the front corner of the building. "Did you see the other two?"

"Yeah, but not much," Baldwin said, panting. "Let's see. They had on reddish bandannas, but everybody's got them. Plain ol' work clothes. The knifer had laced boots like I got. And I don't recall 'em being odd-sized any way. Reg'lar-size men, was all."

"They've disappeared, whatever size they were," Jessie said, frowning while searching the street. "They wouldn't have needed horses, even, just yank down their kerchiefs and mingle. They could've gone on into the Black Nugget, and who'd be the wiser? She turned to Baldwin, asking, "Do just miners buy your kind of boot?"

"No, they're popular with anyone working hard ground, not farms or ranches. So teamsters and road crews and suchlike do, too."

"That hardly narrows it down," Jessie said grumpily. "It's no use, Baldwin. We might as well go back to the Black Nugget."

"I reckon," Baldwin agreed. "Hey, don't I know you?"

Jessie shrugged. "Maybe. How about from the mine?"

"Naw, my boss is a little snippet of a rich gal from Texas who's never set foot in these parts. You do know *me*, though. You called me Baldwin." He stuck out a hand for her to shake, saying, "You can call me Ted."

She took the hand and said, "And you can call me Jessica Starbuck."

"Good enough," Baldwin said. "Pleased to meet you, Miss Star—" He suddenly reddened. "Aw, no, I'm always puttin' my big foot in it. Listen, Miss Starbuck, I'm pure sorry about what I said just now. I was clear mistook about you. Doggone, but it gave me chills, the way you shot that hombre and took out after them others."

112

She shrugged and gave him a broad smile. "Just seemed like a good idea at the time, I guess."

Baldwin scratched his head vigorously. "But who in tarnation was after you? You got any idea about that?"

She realized that now was the opportune moment to bring up the matter she'd been wanting to discuss with him. "Well, I guess we're not all as lucky as Rufus Adams."

His face darkened. "Now what's that s'posed t'mean?"

"That you go gunning for Adams whenever you get drunk enough."

"Who told you anything like that?" he demanded.

"Come on, Ted," she said. "It's not exactly a big secret."

"No, I reckon not," he said, reddening again as he looked down at his feet. But then he looked up again, his eyes hard. "But you mark my words, someday I'll kill that Adams. It's my affair, dammit! What I do is my affair alone!"

"You made it everyone's affair by making it common scandal. You made it mine by working for me—but not working. You drink and gamble and go gunning, and that hurts me. That hurts my manager, too, if he wants to stay a manager and make a go of it."

"I save your life and this is the thanks I get," Baldwin scoffed. "You owe me, but it don't hurt you to forget it."

"I owe you a debt, not charity. I *pay* my debts, too, but not subsidies for nonwork, lost income, padding, embez—"

"All right, all right! P'raps I was lazy and dumb, but I never stole or stuff like that. I won't be no scapegoat for all the muck-up." Baldwin extended his lower lip in a pout. "Don't bother firing me. I quit!" With a truculent snarl, he stormed toward the Black Nugget entrance.

Jessie followed at a more sedate pace. It was resolved. Not as expected, but things rarely are, and she still had the normal loose ends to knot. A new manager to be hired; all books to be audited; the miners to be checked on—God only knew what sort of Baldwin-hired crew she'd inherited—but basically it was resolved, Baldwin no longer a concern or a cost. He could go to hell in a handbasket from here on out, so long as he didn't try to have Starbuck billed for the basket, rope, and one-way travel expenses.

All this passed through Jessie's mind as she reentered the Black Nugget. At the door she met a sorely ruffled Sheriff Meek.

"What's this knifin' an' shootin' ruckus all about?"

"Sheriff, your guess is good as mine." She shrugged, and together they went inside, going on back to the dais, where Baldwin and Chaber were conversing with Nanette and Isabelle.

Nanette greeted Jessie, saying, "We heard you lost 'em."

"We never had them to lose," Jessie replied, and retrieved the impaled violin. Wrenching loose the knife, she saw that it was a plain-handled skinner's type, too ordinary to be identifiable; and failing to find any initials or unique marks, she gave it to the sheriff to ponder. Then, after returning the ruined violin to its downcast owner, she left the dais to go look at the dead man.

On the dais, the violinist was spluttering and Chaber was telling him, "I'll buy you a new fiddle, don't worry." Nanette kept patting an occasionally weepy Isabelle, while Baldwin, too late again, anxiously awaited a chance to take over. Or so it seemed to Jessie, as she looked back when Sheriff Meek called to her.

"Miss Starbuck? Can you identify him?" The sheriff stood on the top step. "Any idea who else? Any enemies trailin' you?"

Jessie lifted the tablecloth that was serving as an impromptu shroud. "No, Sheriff, to all your questions. Not that I know of."

Certainly the corpse was a stranger. A thickset male with stubbly cheeks and the startled expression he'd died with. She lowered the cloth and headed back, not pleased at having killed, but glad that she hadn't been killed instead.

As she neared the sheriff, he said, "Your back was to that door, I understand. Maybe you was mixed up for some other lady."

"That's bound to be it," she agreed with a hint of sarcasm. "Getting murdered by mistake seems the popular favorite hereabouts."

The sheriff began to reply, but was sidetracked by Nanette, who ordered him, "Get off the step. Isabelle wants to get by so she can go to the hotel. Miss Starbuck, you're also a guest, will you see to her?"

Jessie nodded. The sheriff had moved aside and Isabelle was stepping down, but Baldwin jumped from the dais and cut in beside her, tucking her hand under his arm. "Let's go, Miss Isabelle."

With Isabelle between them, Jessie and Baldwin walked over to the French-doored passage to the hotel. Baldwin held the doors, his eyes defying Jessie to interfere. She let him be, glad for his sake to see him showing other interests than booze and gambling.

Reaching the hotel lobby, they saw a dozen, maybe fifteen men encircling Hilliard Latwick. The hotel owner was standing beneath the center chandelier and haranguing his listeners worse than before.

". . . town and countryside have taken enough from one obstinate old rascal!" Latwick was arguing irately. "And I submit that it's high time, *past* high time, us citizens took action to save ourselves!"

"Adams oughta be horsewhipped!" a listener called out.

"Learn him he ain't got no right!" another yelled, not making sense, but not needing to; mobs don't operate on logic or reason. The rest of them milled about, brandishing weapons and shouting similar tripe, fired by Latwick's slanderous tongue-fanning to a burning rage.

Jessie watched Baldwin, wondering if he'd join in or turn away. Baldwin did neither; he stayed put, straddling his fence.

"Madre!" Isabelle suddenly gasped. "She worries sick!"

Descending the stairs was a plump woman on the early side of middle age. She was Mexican, either by birth or one generation removed; and she possessed the same feminine shape and bearing as her daughter. She was wearing a black *camisa,* her prematurely white hair was pinned up, and her face expressed a strength-sapping chronic pain. Yet her resolve to do what needed to be done proved her spirit was as indomitable and unweakened as ever.

Hilliard Latwick had seen the trio enter from the saloon, and now he caught sight of Mrs. Trevarro. Jessie had glimpsed his expressions of surprise, then slyness, and could almost hear the gears meshing as Latwick continued, hands pointing each to a subject.

"Adams had more'n cheated us out of a boom of prosperity, and cheated that young Ted Baldwin's father," Latwick thundered, glaring around. "Now an innercent stranger's been shot dead up near Adams's camp—just 'cause he looked like Adams! Regard his sickly wife and pining child. Who's to blame for these miseries, men?"

"Adams!" came the chorused reply. "Rufe Adams!"

Eyeing Baldwin again, Jessie saw that his face was flushed with alarm and scowling with concern. But he hesitated. He couldn't decide whether he loathed Rufus Adams more or less than he abhorred mob violence. So Jessie figured she'd prepare to lock horns again with Latwick, and damn the consequences. She was spared this by Mrs. Trevarro, who was growing more frantic and furious the more she heard.

116

"What's our duty to murderers, widder an' orphan makers?"

"Hang 'em! Let's get Rufus Adams! Lynch him high!"

Mrs. Trevarro uttered a loud wail. Before it had fully faded, she had a gunbarrel-sized forefinger covering the men. "You don't," she ordered, her voice raspy and thin from her illness. "You mustn't do harm to Rufus Adams. He's not guilty of anything."

"Madam, for all we know, the scoundrel may've pulled the trigger himself," Latwick charged. "In any case, he's responsible."

"No! *Al contrario!*" Mrs. Trevarro raged, wagging her finger at Latwick. "My husband and Rufus Adams, they were half-brothers."

This flabbergasted Latwick, and left him groping for words. His audience was as astonished as he, but not as silenced, and it took a few minutes before the hubbub subsided and she continued.

"*Sí*, same mother, different father," she explained, gazing around with scornfully proud eyes. "That's why they looked some alike. And why Rufus had nothing to do with my husband's death."

Jessie turned to Isabelle, asking, "Didn't you know your father and Rufus were half-brothers? Why didn't you tell us?"

"I knew, of course, but only of him, not where he lives. And nobody asked me or mentioned Uncle Rufus's name. Is he as horrible a thief and badman as I heard?"

"He's guilty of all, and more," Baldwin stated flatly. "Except I won't go believin' offhand rumors of him gunnin' kin. Not Rufus—and I hate him worse'n a hydrophobic skunk."

"Ohh..." Isabelle turned in dismay and darted to her mother. Jessie watched them embrace in the midst of a group of milling and gesturing men who were shouting at Hilliard Latwick, who looked very baffled and embarrassed.

Jessie turned to Baldwin, resisting the temptation to rub in salt, and remarked, "The lynching is fast losing steam, I'd say, but not much in that one bunch around Isabelle and her— Say, isn't that a miner named Lou Quade, from the Snowshoe?"

"Sure is!" Baldwin exclaimed, apparently surprised. "Hey, Lou! Lou Quade! The Snowshoe ain't takin' a hand in this sorta thing. I'll deal with Adams in my own way, so back off! Now!"

Quade shrugged and wandered outside, and that seemed to signal a general desertion. Surprisingly, Hilliard Latwick had calmed down and was apologizing to the Trevarros. Baldwin moved in to plead his own pardons. Jessie was brought over to meet Mrs. Trevarro, who was still trembling with emotion. Mrs. Trevarro said she'd like to retire, and Baldwin insisted on helping Isabelle get her mother up to her room.

Mrs. Trevarro has grit when she needs it, Jessie thought admiringly, while she was glancing up after them. Then, as her gaze moved down around the lobby, Jessie saw Latwick. The hotel man seemed to be still in a quandary of sorts, but if anything permanent ever came of this fray, she hoped it'd be the permanent stuffing of gags into lynch-baiting mouths like Latwick's.

A short while later, Jessie went up to her room. There was still plenty of time before her dinner engagement with Everett Yates, but there were a number of things she wanted to do—including watch the maids iron her dressy suit this time—but mainly she thought.

They had a puzzle, she and Ki. They'd chanced across some of the pieces, and laid bait to hook others, and now she wanted to sort out what they had and get some notion of which pieces were still missing. And make one errand, on the way to dinner.

Chapter 9

In summer, 7:15 P.M. wasn't considered part of evening. There was still plenty of good light for workers to see by, the sun low, yet still continuing its slow decline, sending out scarlet streamers and gilding the distant peaks. The glories of impending evening held little interest for most in Forge, for payday had finally regained some of its hilarity of the morning. The bar trade was booming, the ladies of ill repute had barely had time to lie down on the job, and music and laughter were an earsplitting roar.

But Jessie enjoyed the setting sun as she walked into the trainyard. She found the railroad telegrapher in the depot, already swamped by messages, his clicking telegraph key bringing in more by the minute. Luckily, the telegrapher had an abiding respect for nature, and was so impressed by Jessie's scenic wonders that he felt inspired to wire her message while she waited. It was to the Circle Star Ranch in Texas, and was a short, encoded instruction she'd composed earlier in her room, so the whole deal wasn't as long as she'd feared or he'd hoped.

Then Jessie crossed on through the trainyard to Everett Yates's coach. Crews were still working, she saw, repairing damaged track and clearing away debris, and one group was just finishing placement of the turntable. The shattered roundhouse appeared to need at least one more day to have its roof shored up.

Yates's aide, Virgil, greeted Jessie as sourly as before. This time he was clad in a steward's white mess jacket, and she thought his jaundiced feelings might stem some from the jacket. If she had all his degrees, she'd resent having to work as mess crew.

The coach had been cleaned in her honor, the major miracles having been accomplished in the rear section. The chart table was covered with linen and arranged for two. Coffee-mug vases held sprays of wildflowers, and lo, Everett Yates appeared in an unwrinkled shirt and neat tie.

"Jessie, you're a pip late, just socially perfect," he greeted cheerily. "You look ravishing, far superior to the dinner, I'm afraid."

Dinner was a catered affair, Virgil serving it from the crew mess tent nearby. The food was standard employee fare, meaning it was healthy, plentiful, and often bland— yet rules were that it was fine enough for worker and manager alike. Booze was a perquisite of management, though, and Yates had some wines stashed for just such occasions as this.

Dinner flowed well. Jessie found herself confirming her first impressions of Yates: a shrewd, self-made man, not rich by current standards, but confident enough to hold opinions without being opinionated, and to believe in gambling his abilities against comfortable security. True, he was in his forties, but his type were just hitting their prime then, and she felt his age an attraction.

There was no question that he found her an attraction. Like the telegrapher, Yates was a profound admirer of nature's bounties, preferring bountiful females over natural sunsets. Yet he had sufficiently broad interests that he could appreciate her two-piece outfit of powder-blue Venetian wool, and could recognize it as a creation both stylish and fashionable—two discouraging words rarely heard in Forge.

Afterwards they helped Virgil tidy up. Yates unearthed a half-bottle of brandy, and Virgil asked if he'd care for glasses on the deck. Jessie perked up, asking, "A platform deck?"

"Yes, but no chairs. I sleep there on dry nights."

"Is your cot or bed or whatever fit to be seen?"

"Aye, she's a proper mattress, mum, an' proper clad, too."

Jessie gave a laugh. "Then let's pay her a call."

Bottle in hand, with Virgil trailing behind, Yates ushered Jessie out the rear door. The observation deck was longer than a regular coach vestibule. It was bounded on its three open sides by a waist-high brass rail, and was carpeted with a thick horsehair mattress that was covered in turn with blankets and a navy bedspread.

"Bunks cramp me," Yates said. "This is nice and big."

"Big doesn't always mean respectable," Jessie quipped.

"At what she cost me to be special-made, believe me, she's respectable." He poured brandies, and as Virgil went back in, he gave Jessie a snifter, then toasted and sipped. "Now, where were we? Oh yes, we were talking about you wanting to visit Adams."

"No, after that, about him and Trevarro being half-brothers. No more to tell there. Ted Baldwin quit after we had words. Up to then, he didn't know who I was or that his boss was in town."

"Well, I never told him or anyone much of our plans."

"But it was no great secret, Everett, and wasn't intended to be. Woody Fleishman knew, and those ambushers on our way here certainly knew, so my manager sure should have. It's his business to."

Virgil returned and whispered in Yates's ear, and Yates excused himself for a moment, leaving Jessie alone on the deck. She didn't mind at all, but settled comfortably with her brandy and gazed afar at the burnished gray slopes . . . or lower, at the dusky, lamp-glowing main street . . . or nearer, at the broken wall of the roundhouse, where she could glimpse workmen hoisting the boiler off a damaged loco-motive. And that was how Yates found her when he came back, sitting on the mattress, relaxing dreamily.

"Don't say you're sorry," she said. "I'm not."

He sat down beside her. "All right, I'll just say the coach will jolt in a few minutes. It'll be hooking onto a short freight that's deadheading to rail-end. Why don't you ride along with me?"

"Don't tempt me. I've simply too much work, alas."

"If work includes visiting Adams, he'd be just a skip away. And it's a splendid ride up through the gorge country at night."

"Which reminds me, where would I sleep?"

Yates thought that one over. "Hm," he said, and was still thinking when the coach lurched and swayed. Ahead of the coach was the backing freight, the couplers thundering together and draw-bars grating metallically as the engine hammered the train's tail car against the coach's front.

Sent almost sprawling, Yates regained his balance and tried to reassure Jessie. "It won't bother us. It's not going for a while."

She rose anyway. "I believe I'd better say good night."

"Maybe so. I've nothing left to offer after this," he said

ruefully, standing with the almost empty bottle. "Let's kill it."

Jessie smiled. "All right, I'll split one last drink."

While he carefully measured the brandy into their snifters, Yates sighed and said, "Probably just as well you don't ride along, Jessie. The crews are scared to move without first inspecting everything, and it's about all the foremen can do to keep 'em picking and poking. They're nervous, edgy. Another bomb like today's, and they'll go on general strike."

"If they go, what'll happen to the railroad?"

"Liable to go down. Local investors will sink with it, local culprits will be blamed for it." Moodily, Yates stared down at his drink, swirling it slow and easy as he spoke. "I wonder sometimes just how local. You'll laugh, Jessie, but I sometimes suspect these local fights are somehow part of one huge conspiracy."

Jessie looked at him over the rim of her glass. "Remind me to laugh later. But before I go, I'd like to know why."

"Why? Labor agitators have been planted in my crews, a hard trick that no local could pull. Opium has been smuggled to my Orientals down by Tacoma, which again no local could set up. The same was done to Crocker on his old Central. There's been land-grabbing, political grafting, fraudulent banking, stock manipulating. And it's nothing new, Jessie. I've been running into this kind of thing ever since I first got into railroads. I tell you, I've heard some strange things, most of which I'd hardly credit, except I've seen some things firsthand that's every bit as strange. Like the bank and roundhouse bombing the past couple of days. It's just too damned big and well-organized to be anything local. It's got to be financed by big money—and I do mean *big*."

"Like recognizing an old enemy by its habits, is that it?"

"More like suspecting there's one single enemy by its

habitual methods. One aim, one plot, which I suspect is against our whole transcontinental rail system."

Jessie didn't respond at once, but moved to lean against the deck rail, where she eyed the yard beyond while contemplating all she'd heard.

She remained there until Yates cleared his throat and said, "Well, maybe not. And I admit I can't figure why. It's self-defeating, since there'd be more to exploit from a developing West, and railroads are crucial to such progress. Forget it, Jessie."

"Everett, these same railroads can transfer troops and supplies to anywhere in short order. That is, once they're built to go anywhere." She turned then, and Yates read the genuine concern in her face. "It's militarily vital for a northern rail line to be completed to, say, Tacoma. Until and unless one is, our army and navy will lack the abilities to defend the Pacific Northwest against large, concerted attacks."

He stared at her, a frown furrowing his brow. "My God," he breathed.

The coach shuddered, clanking, a reminder that it was due to depart. Jessie said, "I think I'd better go."

"I suppose." He drained his brandy, then reached across and grasped Jessie's left hand in his. "What's the etiquette on this?"

They stood that way for a few moments; Jessie wasn't thinking of social rules, but of how she'd grown to like him increasingly over the evening. She slid her hand free.

"Everett, I really must go," she insisted.

"Absolutely. And the rule, as I recall, is that I'm to see you off."

"Please do, if it says it's at my pleasure, not your leisure. Well? Are you escorting me up front, or tossing me over back here?"

"Whichever you prefer," he replied agreeably. "Which-

125

ever, I'd prefer to say good night here. I won't have a chance once I toss you out, and Virgil might be still lurking up in the front."

"Fine, first we say good night, then I leave."

"Good night, Jessie."

"Good night," she replied.

He bent over as though to give Jessie a chaste goodnight peck. And she raised her chin to offer her lips for the same. But the kiss that developed was anything but a chaste peck.

Her mouth opened willingly beneath his, to the surprise of both of them. Yates encircled her waist with his hands and tugged her closer to him. Tentatively her arms began to work their way around him, and then their bodies were rubbing against each other while their mouths worked together avidly.

Suddenly the coach jerked their feet out from under them. They landed in a tangle, the coach still shaking a little, their kiss broken and leaving them breathless. Jessie squirmed about to a sitting position, and looked at Yates as if it was all his fault.

"Everett, don't you dare say our powerful kissing knocked us down. I've been on trains enough to know slack being pulled."

"You read my mind, Jessie, and I swear the kisses did it."

"This is silly. What am I doing still on this train?"

"Maybe this will tell you," Yates replied, and he kissed Jessie again, his hand under her chin, pressing her mouth to his.

Jessie was a bit startled to find herself kissing him again, but she was even more astounded by the subtle kick of it. It wasn't demanding or pressuring, nor carnal and lusty. It was warm and very sweet, and it touched something in her that made her feel very good about being kissed by Everett

Yates. And it felt very natural when he enclosed her in his arms again, their knees touching, their position awkward and tiring. But his lips were on hers and she felt very sensual and yet very protected by his strong yet gentle yearning.

She began to feel vibrations then, and realized the train was starting slowly, slowly to move. The train, she sensed, was going a bit faster, and she really must stop this and she would in a second, after she touched the tip of his tongue with hers. It was a hot, sweet touch that made her melt inside.

Jessie then broke the kiss, but remained close enough to feel his hard breathing against her cheek. She whispered, "Everett, let me off this train of yours at once. You are abducting me."

"I'd let you off in an instant, but we're moving too fast."

Jessie turned and stared between the railing bars. They were gathering speed, she could see that, and were passing the dark bulk of the water tower and clattering over the mainline switchpoints. Nobody to cry for help to... even if she'd wanted to.

"I'll have you flogged, Everett, for kidnapping."

"Positively. And probably an extra dose of the lash for dragging you off by the hair, screaming and kicking. But first..."

Tenderly he pushed Jessie down on the platform mattress, then lay beside her, perched on his elbow. He put his lips on hers softly, searchingly, and ran his tongue over her lips and pushed into her mouth to find rich heat. Jessie wriggled, sighing, squirming into a more comfortable position, settling herself down to luxuriate in his caress.

There was no more talking for a long while. Yates was gentle, treating Jessie as if she were very fragile, very dear. He moved closer to her, putting the weight of his chest on her, placing his hands under her shoulders, and pressing her close. The kiss became a deep thing now, wet, intimate, intense. She accepted and returned his mouth pressure, eyes closed, letting the sweet thrill of it soak into her flesh.

Jessie started moaning and quivering, squirming as his fingers molded her sensitive breasts and found, under the tightness of her suit jacket and blouse, one of her nipples and teased it into vivid awareness . . . and they both knew it was time to remove all hindrances to their yearning bodies.

"I want to," he murmured. "Like an onion."

Jessie smiled and lay back, enjoying the touch of his dexterous fingers. She leaned one way, then the other, raising her arms to help him remove her jacket. Then her blouse went too, and Yates smiled as he stared at her thrusting breasts and dark, jutting nipples, giving each a kiss and moving on.

Kneeling, unfastening her skirt, Yates pushed it over her arching pelvis and down her legs. Jessie helped kick it aside, leaving it with her shoes in a puddle on the mattress. She wasn't wearing a petticoat this time, there being only so much space in her small traveling case; but she had on a fine set of pantalettes, made of Valenciennes lace and nearly translucent silk. Yates had a bird's-eye view of the golden-red delta between her thighs as he untied the drawstring and eased her pantalettes along her legs.

"Stunning, truly stunning," he murmured, and drew into almost a Moslem prayer position, bending forward to bow his head at the shrine between her legs. He kissed her upper thigh, worming higher and more toward the inside. When he shifted slightly, she gasped and stiffened in reflex. It had the effect of pushing her deeper into his wet caress, and a shaft of pure delight shot through her at his moist, open-mouthed touch. Nude, on a train's observation deck. Breasts firm, nipples painfully swollen. Her legs open, forced open by his palms. He was doing exquisite things to her body, thrilling things that caused her to squirm with tense pleasure. Then, inevitably, he came to her.

Yates tore off his clothing. Jessie eyed his bare form as appreciatively as he had studied hers. He was silhouetted in the softly falling dusk, as the train continued riding through a seemingly endless succession of canyons and tiered slopes; and Jessie thought the naked man fit his surroundings well. His shoulders were wide, his hips solid, and the muscles across his torso looked firm, though not the rock they'd been in his youth. But youth had been made up for by tempering experience, making Everett a prime combination of strength and maturity.

And virility, Jessie noticed with something akin to trepidation.

And when he pressed close alongside her, Jessie reveled in the heat of her breasts against his chest, and could feel heat elsewhere at his fondling touch. While his left hand toyed almost idly with her nipples, his right one vanished. She gasped when she felt it slide over her crotch, his finger tracing up and down its seam, testing the silky softness of her delta, finding the center of her passion with a practiced finger, and pressing and rolling it gently.

Sighs and low moans erupted from her mouth. She shuddered hard, passion sparking through her until she was ready to plead for him to stop teasing. Then he did stop, and she wanted more.

Leaving her breast, Yates backed away and pushed between her legs. She watched the look on his face as he guided his thick, pulsating manhood forward.

Jessie opened her legs wide, sprawling and spreading lasciviously, feeling his staff deep inside her moist furrow, throbbing and searching out every fold, every hidden nook and cranny. He paused then, lying upon her and pressing her breasts. Jessie pressed against him in return, and their eyes met, smiling, and he slowly began pumping.

"Yes," she sighed, eyes closing. "Let's make steam..."

Yates quickened his tempo with long, sawing strokes. There was only marginal yield to his mattress, and none to the hard flooring beneath. He kept on pounding her, and she kept demanding more.

Jessie's head rocked back and forth and her eyes rolled upward. She felt it—God, how she felt it! Surely Everett possessed a full yard of gliding, throbbing, dilating, hard metal rail, hot as fire, that forced wide her loins and drilled her wet depths!

But her body was not intimidated.

Her yearning belly tried to swallow Yates whole.

Her taut buttocks were buffeted against the mattress by his stormy hammering. Straining hard, he plunged all the way into her wetly distended channel, gasping and panting with his straining urgency, his spiraling desire.

Jessie moaned beneath him, trying to match his insatiable beat. She listened to his hard breathing, then felt his hand sliding down between their bellies, lower until one finger was caressing her clitoris. The combination of the strokings was too much for her already emotion-torn senses. Her mouth filled his ears with inarticulate little cries. She could feel the swaying of the coach beneath her, as its steel wheels clacked over the rail joints at an ever-increasing tempo, in time to Yates's ever more powerful thrusts.

"Ahhh, Lord!" Jessie wept, biting her lip, her nails raking Yates's back. The engine's whistle gave a long, shrill scream—or did it come from Jessie?—as she felt the railroad man shudder, his warm eruption spewing far up inside her. Then her own inner muscles spasmed, tightening around his pulsing shaft.

They came together like a pair of colliding engines, and

her passion exploded like a locomotive's boiler at full steam.

They may have been rolling through the hills near Forge, but Jessie called it paradise . . .

Chapter 10

Jessie was not prepared for the full impact of the dramatic scene awaiting her at end-of-track. Leaving Yates's private coach at daybreak, she found herself witnessing the actual laying of rails on which transcontinental trains could haul freight, mail, and passengers across northern America.

Sledges hammered rhythmically in triple time, ten spikes to the rail. Hard-pressed to keep pace with this hefty anvil chorus, other crews hustled up track sections and aligned them on crossties, which tie-laying crews had set and leveled in the ballasted grade. Single-horse lightcars rolled at a gallop with loads of sections, to be tipped off-track as soon as they were emptied, allowing full cars to advance while they dashed back to reload.

Astride a splotched pinto mare, Jessie rode the length of this intense, fast-charged, racketing operation. There was a sense of urgency and importance to the work, which made it harder to remember that the PS&C might not turn out to be a moneymaking concern. Transcontinental trains *could*, not necessarily *would*, use it, and even that depended on the Northern Pacific building up this way.

Jessie also found difficulty in finding the labor unrest that Yates had come to handle. All the crewmen she saw looked to be working as quickly and forcefully as possible, which she thought was amazing, considering this was the day after payday. To be fair, Everett had claimed that the slowdowns were mainly among the construction crews, who worked some distance ahead of rail-end. He'd be with them today, he'd told her, where they were excavating a cut.

She continued flanking the right-of-way past the spikers and rail-layers, and shortly came to the tie-laying crews, who gave her a cheer as she loped by. The new gravel roadbed stretched on into the uplands, but very soon Jessie swung off onto a dirt path. The path wasn't much, and kept close to the contours of the hills, rarely along ridges, but through clefts and hollows. Originally it had been a game trail, she surmised, that eventually was used more by humans. And the only reason she was using it now was that Everett had insisted it was a shortcut.

The path was included in Yates's directions, which he'd given Jessie much earlier, around dawn. He'd also borrowed a horse and gear, and since her fine outfit made anything like straddling a horse impossible, he'd scrounged up some work clothes for her to wear. The only worker near her size was a young chef's helper, and at that she had to roll up the cuffs and pull in the waist.

So she wasn't surprised to be cheered by the tie-laying crew. She knew how she looked. Some women would look like pixies or innocent little waifs in such a getup. She still looked every inch a Starbuck, only somehow trapped in a clown's pantaloons.

Shortly the path intersected a larger wagon trail—the

Moon Trail, assuming that Yates's instructions were correct. She turned onto it and headed northeast, not expecting to recognize anything along the trail, because this had to be way past the pocket canyon where she'd stopped with Ki. But it was about where the trail should logically be, and it felt like the meandering course the trail preferred, squiggling toward an increasingly rugged country of tumbling creeks and thickly forested slopes.

The sun had just passed into midmorning when the trail capped a knoll and declined sharply along meadowed steppes into the maw of a wide, inviting canyon. Jessie slowed, almost reined in once, and when she entered the canyon, she rode down its center.

This was it, she knew. Concealed in rock-ribbed timberland, this was the Moon Trail Canyon of nightrider fame. Killed on the canyon's trail had been a nightriding relative of the canyon's owner. It was worth sharing a few words over. Maybe Rufus Adams didn't want to face questions or learn answers, but Jessie had been feeling increasingly that she should make an effort to find out.

Gradually the sides closed in, becoming more weathered and rotten, with numerous blotches of deserted prospecting burrows. Eventually it funneled into what was virtually a ravine, an elongated bottleneck that stretched some distance ahead before widening back out again. And all along the high ridges grew so many trees that the impression was of one single entity sheared down its middle by the bisecting canyon trail.

Finally the canyon began widening, its sides continuing a gradual leaning away and lowering as well. Only once, sharply and briefly, did they draw close together again, and then they seemed to converge almost into one unbroken cliff. It wasn't quite, for it was there that Jessie saw the signpost and secondary trail.

The signpost consisted of an old warped front door nailed to a proper-sized peeled log. It was set up beside the secondary trail, which cut away toward an easily overlooked canyon offshoot; and painted on the sign was an arrow pointing that way, and the single word ADAMS in letters too big to overlook easily.

Hesitating, Jessie glanced ahead up Moon Canyon. Not too far beyond, in some grubby back-pocket gulch, lay her Snowshoe Mines. Farther on, past Adams's property line, camped railroad survey and construction engineers planning where and how the rails should go.

Nowhere, Jessie thought as she veered onto the secondary trail. *To a dead stop nowhere, if Adams can't be brought around.*

The deeply rutted wagon track went pretty straight through some rock outcroppings and wooded groves, and Jessie thought she could detect the noisy paralleling course of a hidden white-water tributary nearby. Soon the track began wandering in and out of steepening culverts and ridge-flanking groves, until finally it got tangled in a dense forest and dribbled to an end at the far end of the forest.

A clearing was there, a big one hewn from the forest. The stream she'd heard ran through it, and buildings were set at intervals along the banks. The main house was a comfortable but ordinary box of four rooms, and the bunkhouses, outbuildings, and corrals were typical of thousands of such structures throughout the West. Nothing appeared opulent or to have much paint on it, but it'd look plush compared to the temporary tent camps the logging crews lived in when working the woods. Which was where they probably were now, she guessed. They certainly weren't here, and not much of their equipment, either.

Drawing near the house, she saw two men on its front porch. She dismounted by a corral fence, a short walk away, and recognized the man who was standing as one of the Pace twins, though she couldn't tell which one. The other was sitting in a wicker easy chair, and she'd identified him by voice long before observing his face. It was Rufus Adams.

"I warned Cervant I'd shoot the next miner who did that!" Adams was hollering, his brows beetling. "Somebody'll pay dear!"

Approaching, Jessie heard too little to figure out the story. Now, though, she could see that Adams had his right foot propped on a stool, and much of his leg sandwiched in a clumsy splint made out of what looked like crate slats and bedsheet strips. She reached the porch in time to make sense of the Pace boy's next report:

"Watchdog fell in that deep blind hole over by the line," the boy was saying. "I dunno if they'll find her in time."

"You left her down there? That dumb, drunken mutt?"

"Well, sure, she's Snowshoe's. Kinda evens it, too."

"You don't hit back at folks by hurtin' their animals, however deservin' they might be!" Adams roared, raising and swinging a wooden cane. "Hightail yer ass back there and haul her out!"

"Hey! Awright!" The boy fled off the porch.

"Bring her back here for soberin'!" Adams bellowed after him, then caught sight of Jessie, stared, and gestured hospitably. "Didn't rec'lect you in them duds, ma'am, and still don't know your name."

Moving closer, Jessie introduced herself and said she had two reasons for coming: "One of them you'll be glad to hear. I own the Snowshoe, and want to work out any problems you and it have."

"What?" Adams gaped at her. "A *lady* owns that cesspool? The millennium is at hand!" Then he said, in a quieter tone, "I got a grievance list that'll curl your ears, not the

136

least bein' drunkard watchdogs and waterbeds fouled with coal waste. But the only real answer is to flatten it and sow the earth with salt."

"Come now, Mr. Adams, I haven't seen it yet, but—"

"You ain't? No wonder you'll admit to ownin' it. Tell you what, you go see the mine, and then we'll talk. Well, you promised two reasons, the first gladifyin'. The next ain't?"

"More saddening. I do wish to convey my condolences."

"Thanks kindly, I'll savor 'em, first death I get."

"But..." Jessie paused unsurely, then sighed. "Oh dear, you haven't been told. It's your half-brother, Eugene Trevarro. He died the night before last, and was taken to Sneed's, in Forge."

"You're crazy! I wrote Gene in Nogales only two months ago!"

"He must've been coming to see you. He was killed on Moon Trail, and his widow and daughter are still in town." Quickly, Jessie gave Adams the main points and the old lumberman listened in stricken silence, his eyes wide with horror, until she was through.

"Stubborn fool," he said heavily. "I wrote him to stay till I could scrape the money together and send it to him. Connie—his wife, Consuela—needs an operation, and natcherly I wrote him he could borrow from me for it. But I had to raise it first."

"Isabelle said she'd been told nothing about any of it."

"That's Gene, close-mouthed as a clam," Adams said, harsh anger welling up, raising his voice to a bitter yell. "Now Gene'll never say nothin' more. On account of a certain spavined timber wolf who crosseyed him for me!"

"D'you have any idea who?"

"Yates," Adams snapped. "Who else? He's got everything ridin' on tracks through Moon Trail Canyon, and I

137

stopped him solid. He's got reason and guts to go gunnin'. Well, so do I!"

"You don't think Ted Baldwin's involved?"

Adams snorted. "Not lest he won a backbone at cards. All he can stomach is drinkin' and gamblin' away what his dad left him."

"Just what was your deal with Ted's dad?"

"Ain't none of your concern, Miss Starbuck." Adams eyed her belligerently, then softened. "Weren't your concern to come tell me 'bout Gene, though, so p'raps a swap's fair. Well, Zack Baldwin didn't have no money, but he had big ideas and big tastes and big bills to me. When he was dyin' slow, he deeded me his canyon, figurin' it'd pay me back more than if he willed it to me after he died, and the legal hyenas tore into his leavings. There was only one dumb condition, and I think we were drunk when we stuck it in. Zack and his son got ten years to repay my debts in full, and get the canyon back."

"You said you stuck it in, like in a contract?"

"Well, it's on paper, all signed an' sealed. I'll allow it weren't the slickest deal I've made. But young Ted couldn't raise the cash if he had a *hundred* years. Meantime, I can't sell or give away the canyon, but hafta keep it in a kinda trust for, oh, six more years."

"So that's why you won't sell a right-of-way!"

"Sure, I can't," Adams said bluntly. "I'll only lease 'em one at my price, but they insist on buying, and it got my dander up, so t'hell with them. 'Nough foolish talk. I'm goin' to town."

"Wait!" Jessie pleaded. "It's too dangerous for you to go. Feeling's running high against you, and we barely succeeded in breaking up a lynch mob last night that was gathering against you."

"I dunno what they're so proddy about, but ain't enough men in Forge to hang me!" Adams retorted loudly. "I gotta take care of my own flesh an' blood. I gotta give Gene a decent burial afore he's planted on boot hill, an' I gotta bring the womenfolk back here to live. Dadgum it, woman, stop hinderin' a man's doin's!"

"At least take two or three men along."

"I'll do nothin' of the sort!" Adams howled indignantly. "They got work to do, and I didn't have to tell you this much, and I ain't gonna tell you no more! Pack on outta here, Miss Starbuck, and tend to your own trimmings!"

Sensing she'd stretched it as far as she could, Jessie began rising to leave. Adams was struggling to stand up, but was mostly flopping and falling back.

"Busby!" Adams kept shouting. "Busby, get out here!"

"Right, boss," answered a voice from inside the house.

"Get me up! Hitch up the wagon, I'm going to Forge!"

"Sorry, boss, the wagon's busted."

"The wagon's not busted!" Adams thundered, struggling.

"Sure is, boss. Yesterday it busted a wheel, same time you dumped it over and busted your leg. You remember."

The old lumberman looked as though he were about to explode. "Then *fix* the wagon! Get somebody to, and clean up the house!" he ordered, managing to hobble upright. "Soon's I get this contraption off and into town, I'll kill me the skunk who shot Gene, and then I'm bringin' two ladies home with me!"

Jessie hastened to her horse, not wishing to be caught in the crossfire of raving and ranting. It looked as though she had stirred up a hornet's nest in visiting Rufus Adams, but she didn't regret it. She'd learned a few things, such as that Adams had a strong sense of fairness, and wasn't the grasping, selfish villain everyone seemed to believe. She'd learned a few other things, and still more things were falling in place.

One thing was clear, though. Things were going to pop in Forge, as soon as Adams got his wagon aimed that way.

Chapter 11

"If that old devil comes after *me* with a gun," Everett Yates declared confidently, "he'll be raising his last rumpus."

"There you go at loggerheads," Jessie rebuked. "The same tactics you two have been using all along, forcing and more forcing."

"I used pressure, what I had, that's only good business. Besides, the railroad means too much to everyone in the region to risk taking half-measures. Look there! Should Adams force us to stop?"

There, where Jessie was to look, was directly ahead at a beetling wall of rock. Construction crews were making a cut through it wide enough to accommodate the main track and a siding, and she'd been looking there almost consistently since her arrival at the site, around noon. Not much else to look at, she soon found: a horse path near the rock, the rough right-of-way stretching back to rail-end, the flanking dense woods—

And Everett Yates, who'd been here as he'd said he'd

be, quite satisfied with his day so far. His labor troubles were over, she gathered, Yates having agreed to post more night watchmen and to let the men keep weapons—which some had already been doing, either packing sidearms or propping carbines within reach. What good they were against hidden bombs was never explained to Jessie. Yates didn't want it even asked, as long as the men were working.

And working they were.

At the base of the rock, steam shovels tore up huge masses of talus; the puffing of their engines and the thudding of their shovels, dumping earth and rock into six-wheel wagons, echoed and reverberated within the construction site, mingling with the chattering of steam drills and the hammering of hand drilling heads. Gangs of men with picks and shovels were busy clearing debris or grading the right-of-way, while, higher on the wall, the drillmen bored holes to receive powder charges that would bring down more of the cliff face.

Jessie, astride the pinto, with Yates mounted alongside on a ring-eyed dun, watched the operation and knew what Yates meant. "Adams hasn't the force to stop a railroad, Everett, and the opportunities, the new and better things, the progress it'll mean. He just doesn't have the right to sell you his land. And you're just as bad about stopping things, when you don't want to take a lease. Have you ever wondered," she asked, shaking her head sadly, "if your feud with Adams might have drawn in others? Have you thought that maybe an outsider might have been attracted, and could be using you for his own ends?"

"Who?"

Jessie shook her head, reading Yates's mind. "Not Ted Baldwin. If anybody's being used as tools and scapegoats, it's you two, because you've got the baldest reasons to hate Adams."

Yates opened his mouth to respond—but what he said

was never heard. It was drowned in a roaring explosion that seemed to cause even the adamant stone of the cut to quake and reel.

Through a mushrooming cloud of yellowish smoke, Jessie could see splintered framing and twisted steel beams, ripped sections of a steam-shovel cab and boiler plates and rock flying in all directions. Her pinto gave a prodigious snort, rising on its hind legs, while Yates's dun crawfished in pure terror. It was all Jessie and Yates could do to keep their mounts from wheeling and bolting back down the cut.

As the smoke cloud began to rise, thinning out, Jessie perceived a hole in the ground where the shovel had stood, and all around, men were lying motionless or were tottering, bloody and dazed. The uninjured were still numbed to senselessness, and were lurching around bewildered, too disorganized to be of much help.

Jessie took one glance at the stunned confusion around her, and yelled to Yates, "Come on, we've got to rally them!"

Yates leaned closer, cupping his ear, still deafened by the explosion. Jessie signaled him to follow her, and heeled the pinto into a gallop toward the scene of the disaster. Yates kicked his dun forward, a nose-length behind.

But scarcely were the horses in stride when a volley of rifle fire seared through the hazy smoke. Bullets ripped by, mere inches away, concentrating on Jessie and Yates because they were the only ones on horseback. But not for long. There was an ugly *splat!* as Jessie's pinto took a slug, shuddered once, and started to fall. Jessie flung herself clear as the animal went down, thrashing and whinnying.

"Get off!" she shouted at Everett. "Get down, you're a prime target up there!" Then, to the workers milling nearby, she called, "Get cover! If you got guns, grab them!" Taking her own advice, Jessie plunged for concealment.

142

More guns were opening fire now. Except for a few workers bereft of brains, everyone dove in a chaotic rout for shelter behind boulders, machinery, stacks of supplies, or whatever was close.

Hugging the earth under one of the six-wheel wagons, Jessie searched for the source of the attack. Her first notion was the flanking woods above, but a bearded workman bellied up beside her, and used his carbine to point toward the right-of-way.

"Gawd, it's like Injuns attackin'!"

In a sense he was right, Jessie thought, but Indians weren't this rash. Eighteen, perhaps twenty riders were streaming in to strike from the rear, wildly outnumbered by crewmen and with only two ways to get out. They were figuring on surprise and on the workers still being shocked dimwitted—both of which, Jessie had to admit—were appallingly true. But she wondered if they were also counting on the workers being unarmed—which was mostly true, and those who had weapons may not have taken them to cover.

Yates dove in on Jessie's other side, saying, "Not a spare gun to be found!" Then he winced, biting dirt, as a bullet nearly parted his hair.

The attackers split at the last moment into two curving waves that surged along the side lanes used by the wagons. With only trees to the outside, they could concentrate their lethal mayhem on the workers trapped in the middle, and they poured in salvos, bullets riddling tools and equipment, and ricocheting off rubble left from the cut.

The man beside Jessie grunted, licked his thumb, and fired. He hit one rider in the breastbone, and was tracking a second when he grunted and collapsed. Jessie glanced over and saw his suddenly sprouted third eye, and wormed his old, battered Winchester out of his grasp. Pressing her

143

cheek against its stock, she lost no time in picking up where he'd left off, dropping another rider out of his saddle. She rolled, levering, to find a third.

Increasingly, the workers who had weapons were opening up, as the attackers swept farther along the sides. From the haphazard defense could be heard the throaty blasts of .50-90 Express rounds, and the sharper cracks of repeaters like Jessie's. Flanking them were pounding hooves and the drumming reports of .56-60 Spencer carbines, which the riders seemed to prefer. Some now could be spotted using glow-punks to ignite sticks of black powder, then hurling them with fuses sparking into the midst of the sheltering construction equipment.

It was a bold plan, Jessie realized in that instant. Destroy the machines and specialty tools, and the jobs were wiped out, even if the workers decided they wanted them. Assuming any workers would be alive to choose, after this blasting!

As fearfully aware as Jessie, the armed workmen focused their firepower on the riders with powder sticks. One of the horses fell, throwing its rider, who sprinted away with a zigzagging gait, leaving his stick under his fallen horse. A second powderman ignored the gunfire, lobbed his stick well into the air, then ripped rein and galloped to catch up with the others.

Twin eruptions geysered flame and thunder, the detonations echoing resounding through the cut. The dead horse was blown into the air, transformed into several large pieces of bloody meat. A tie-loaded car near the second steam shovel was smashed into kindling and iron, and a worker using it as cover was hurled out of his boots, collapsing like an empty sack.

More powdermen veered away from the twin lines of attackers, braving furious rifle fire to fling their sticks. Two were downed in time, but others got through, and explosions rocked the floor of the cut, spewing men and materiel, spreading death and destruction—but never silencing the workers' defiant guns.

Smoothly the marauding riders melded into a single galloping file as they arrived at the front, near the rock wall. Flowing together without hesitation or awkwardness, they fled swiftly up the horse path and vanished noisily into the trees.

Workers boiled out from behind their blast-ravaged cover, shouting and cursing, utterly demoralized. Jessie, with Yates grimacing beside her, surveyed the ghastly carnage of human and animal bodies. A good half of the attackers were dead, a heavy price for success. The raid was that, unquestionably.

"Come on, Everett, we've got work to do," she said with grim urgency. "There are a lot of wounded to take care of."

Yates nodded, exhaling heavily. "That's all that's left."

Jessie said nothing to that, not knowing what to say. She turned away, hearing faintly, from beyond the screen of rock and forest, the drumming of many hooves receding northeastward into remote Cascade country.

Chapter 12

When Ki awoke that morning, it was already daylight. He rarely slept so late, especially in strange places—and this place was definitely strange, in more ways than one. On the other hand, he was rarely as exhausted as he'd felt last night.

Dressing, he descended to the first floor and, finding no one around, went out the rear door to the stable. His roan appeared much more chipper now, and Ki quickly saddled and led it outside, then mounted and started to swing toward the wagon trail.

It was then that he glimpsed Jericho, his bald head shining in the sunlight, trudging in the opposite direction a short distance away. He had Valerie's wolf-dog on a chain leash, and the dog clearly did not like it—no more than Jericho, Ki concluded from the scene, must like taking the dog out for a morning constitutional.

Urging his horse into motion, Ki rode toward Forge

through the pale gold of early sunlight.

He found the town quiet enough upon his arrival. Drained after a night of payday debauch, it presented a drowsy, bucolic picture, marred slightly by some leftover drunks and the gutted bank building. Ki stopped by the hotel first and, after determining that Jessie wasn't in, stayed long enough to wash up, check his wound, and change shirts. Then he turned in his horse at the livery, saw that Jessie's roan was there, and walked down to the trainyard.

Gone was the private coach of E. E. Yates.

Smiling faintly, Ki went back to the main street and ate a late breakfast. He walked it off by going to Woody Fleishman's freightyard, up at the other end of town, but the clerk in the office said Mr. Fleishman wasn't back from a run yet. So Ki returned to the Black Nugget, where he encountered Nanette in the saloon.

Nanette wasn't busy and was in a mood to gab. Ki listened attentively as she recounted yesterday's sneak attack on Jessie, the resultant fight, and the identification of Adams's half-brother.

"Isabelle and her mother are worried, can't blame 'em, but once they move in, I can watch out for them good," Nanette said firmly. "It'll be up to me alone, too, while George is gone."

"Oh? I was hoping to see Chaber today."

"You just missed him, Ki. He went to his room saying he wouldn't be around for a spell, and that may mean most anything, from ten minutes to a week. You never can tell when George will show up." Nanette eyed Ki anxiously, slowly shaking her head. "Y'know, I think you and that nice Miss Starbuck are awful foolhardy to be mixing in this, whatever this is, without a law badge backing you. The more I see of you, the more I'd hate to see something happen."

Ki grinned roguishly. "Going to miss me when I'm gone?"

"I darn well could," Nanette admitted candidly, and kissed him solidly on the mouth. Turning, eyes atwinkle, she walked away without another word, never glancing back.

Licking his lips, Ki left through the French doors to the hotel. Pausing at the desk, he doodled on a piece of paper, folded it, and told the clerk it was a message for George Chaber. When the clerk put his note in one of the pigeonholes, Ki glimpsed the room number and the lack of a key. So he sauntered out and across the street, where he lounged against a shop wall and waited for Chaber to leave his room, his key, and the hotel.

He'd been standing there for a half hour, when Chaber appeared and hurried up the street with purposeful steps. Ki moved after him, abandoning for the moment his initial intention of searching Chaber's room. Chaber had the reputed habit of riding off and disappearing at odd times. From the man's manner, Ki felt sure this must be one of those times, and he was all primed to ride a tag on Chaber, no matter how far it took him.

Trouble was, the livery stable was the other way.

Chaber continued on up, frequently glancing around in that nonchalant manner of his. Ki couldn't figure out whether the man was being warily alert or mildly curious, but he took pains to drift along a number of paces behind, keeping to the shadows of overhangs and roofs. He saw Chaber cross to the front of the druggist's, pause at its far corner to gaze idly about, then slip into the alley.

Ki broke into a sprint, reaching the corner mere seconds after Chaber. He took one swift look along the alley, just in time to see Chaber stepping across the staircase landing, and the door up there opening to let him in. The door snapped closed, but Ki stared at it a bit longer, and started to chuckle.

148

This was definitely not something he'd have thought of George Chaber. Or of Martha, for that matter. But as Ki walked back down toward the Black Nugget, he considered it some more, and found it less amusing. Martha had once had a penchant for outlaw lovers. Maybe her past wasn't quite over.

Reaching the hotel, he collected his key and went upstairs. The landing was midway along the main corridor, where a branch corridor joined it like the tail of a T. Ki went along the main corridor, and was starting to unlock his door when he saw Ted Baldwin reach the landing, turn confusedly for an instant, then move into the branching corridor. Ki yanked out his room key and pivoted to lightfoot after the young man, but no more got his back to the door when it swept open.

Ki whirled, and glimpsed the forms of two men in his dim room. The blinds were drawn, so he couldn't discern their features, but he couldn't mistake their actions—one was gripping the knob of the door he'd wrenched wide, while the closer man was looming out at Ki, his arm raised high, gripping a butcher knife.

With reflexes honed by his years of training, Ki moved in, catching the man's knife-wielding arm on the backswing, before he had a chance to bring the blade forward. Using this momentum, he bent the man backwards and, bringing his other hand into play, used its stiffened fingers in a spearhand blow to the killer's Adam's apple. He was rewarded by the satisfying crunch of cartilage as the man's windpipe was crushed.

With a startled expression, the man made a gagging sound and continued to arch over backwards, dropping the knife with a clatter. The first part of his body to strike the floor was his head, with a jarring thud that would probably have killed him, but he was on his way to death already, his shattered windpipe hemorrhaging into his lungs.

Ki leaped over the fallen body to get at the other man, but he was too late. The second man was sliding out through the room's window, only his hands and shirtcuffs showing how he was escaping, one hand on the ledge and the other clutching the upraised sash. While springing after him Ki knew it was futile; the man must have started to flee even before he'd seen his partner dead.

The man let go of ledge and sash, but got the window-shade cord tangled in his fingers or cuff snap. He went down and so did the blind, ripping off its roller to flap out like a flying tail. There was a hollow thump just as Ki reached the window, and peering out, he saw a narrow overhang that spanned the rear of the hotel. Loping across the back field toward the trees, the man was angrily wrestling with the blind, otherwise seeming no worse for having dropped to the overhang, and then to the ground.

Ki closed the window in furious silence and returned to examine the knifer. His trained reflexes had again saved his life, but in retrospect he wished he'd managed to hold back this time, to hurt instead of kill this man, and learn a few answers.

"Hey!" a voice exclaimed. "Hey, that's Lou Quade!" Ted Baldwin lunged up alongside Ki, almost stumbling over the body.

"Easy," Ki said, glancing up at the young man. "He was trying to knife me, and look what with—a butcher knife."

"Why, that murderin' snake!" Baldwin declared, then peered down to observe Ki's actions. "Hey, now what're you doing?"

Ki ripped open Lou Quade's shirt to reveal an empty knife sheath at the man's waist. "Was Quade a knifer?"

"Well, I dunno. I never myself saw him in action, though some of the boys said he was good, and he preferred 'em to guns." Baldwin shook his head, patently mystified. "Is that why you opened his shirt? Did you know he had that empty sheath on him?"

"Actually, I was looking for something else," Ki replied, standing thoughtfully. "But I'm not surprised to find the sheath."

"*I'm* surprised. Here I go lookin' for Miss Starbuck—"

"That's what you were doing up here? Looking for her room?"

"I wanted a couple more words with her, but that ain't the point. Here I come along and find you and one of my ol' miners killin' each other for no good reason I can see, no reason atall."

"Don't worry about it. The few ideas I have don't add up, except for my good reason of self-defense. I'd better be telling the sheriff that, too. Miss Starbuck's not in, but stick around."

"Ain't necessary," Baldwin said, and shuddered. "I'd rather help you as your eyewitness, all the same."

Ki went down to the lobby, Baldwin dogging his heels, and reported the event to the clerk. With a warning to make sure everything stayed put for the sheriff, Ki and Baldwin left the clerk and hurried over to the sheriff's office. They found Sheriff Meek in, perusing a pink-papered copy of the *Police Gazette*.

The sheriff greeted them, "So who got killed an' how bad?"

"No joke," Ki began, but that was as far as he got. An engine had roared into the trainyard, pulling flatcars of badly injured men, and runners from there came bursting in to bring the sheriff, while others raced to fetch Dr. Elgin.

Once again the trainyard was a loud melee of rubber-necking townspeople. There was nothing much for them to do except stand gawking and gossiping, which they managed to do with great intensity and fervor. Rather, Ki realized as he wedged through to the train, it was the railroad workers whose behavior had changed.

Some workers were helping litter certain of the injured. A few others guarded the half-dozen wounded attackers, who were mutely grimacing in pain and brooding over their fate. But, like the townsfolk, the majority had nothing to do. They stood in tense groups, shaking their heads, pointing and muttering, making no effort to resume their jobs. The foremen did not attempt to get them back on the job, either, acting as if they also had lost stomach for returning to the railhead.

In short order, Ki located Jessie on one of the flatcars, tending to victims with what paltry supplies were at hand. He hardly recognized her. Disheveled, in tentlike shirt and oversized jeans, blood smudging her face, dirt and grit embedded in her tousled hair, Jessie was far from her usual elegant self.

"What happened?" Ki asked.

She smiled wearily. "Plenty."

It took Ki a while to persuade Jessie to leave. But she truly wasn't needed here now; there were many willing others who could readily handle the wounded and other loose ends. But there was much for her to do elsewhere, the first thing being to give her account of the attack to Sheriff Meek.

Ten minutes later, after Yates had also been summoned, the four were convened in Yates's coach. "Undoubtedly the steam shovel exploding and the riders' charge were coordinated," Yates said, concluding his and Jessie's detailed report. "That requires timing, and timing in this instance means traitors in my crew."

"It had to have been arranged days earlier, the bomb or whatever detonated the shovel rigged to explode at a definite time," Jessie added, nodding. "I can't believe the raiders would've attacked if they'd known some of the workmen were armed. That started this morning."

"Thank the good Lord you did have weapons," Sheriff Meek growled. "But it'd been planned to be a massacre. So it's come to that, has it?" He was standing motionless, his eyes burning like dark ingots in his rigid face. "Next they'll be slaughterin' us in our sleep. If only we could catch up with them Red Devils."

"Maybe," Ki said speculatively. "Maybe we can."

Yates gestured dismissively. "We can't. They've long gone."

"To the northeast, from what I heard," Jessie said.

"Gawd, I'm an old fool, I can't even get the right way they go," Sheriff Meek groaned. "I've kept reckoning Green River way."

"Sheriff, twice you've chased the Devils that way, and the last time we found their prints on the crest," Ki said. "So you've got proof you're right, and that the general direction they take is southwest. So why would they head northeast, if it wasn't to trick us? So we'd go that way, or give it up as hopeless, while they double back?"

"That's swallerin' a gawdalmighty wad o' ifs."

"No, that part does fit," Yates contended. "They couldn't go straight back, because the railroad and wagon trails more or less do, and because Forge is along that same line. Knowing these hills a mite, Sheriff, I'd say they couldn't simply skirt around a little. They'd have to make a ferociously long curve, and some weaseling at that, and they'd need to buy time."

"Still, presumin' all your assumin's," the sheriff countered, "don't mean we can find their roost any better than we done before."

"Yesterday I went back and managed to trace those prints from the crest a little farther. All right, I admit I don't have

153

them pinned down exactly yet, but I'm following a hunch I think will get us close enough, in the hills a few miles north of the trail."

"Y'mean to try a raid?"

"They have a start on us, but we may still run 'em down."

"What if we fail? If you're wrong, and we miss 'em?"

"We can't fail worse than we are by sitting here. But if we're going to try, let's try it now. We've no time to waste."

The sheriff grinned and touched his revolver. "You're right, son. It's graspin' at a straw, but it's the only straw we got, so we can't be too modest about givin' it our damnedest. Lemme round up a posse quick, and we'll ride!"

They trooped out of the coach, Yates determined to be included. Yates also, to Jessie's delighted surprise, came to her defense when the sheriff wanted to disallow her coming along:

"I witnessed her in action, Sheriff, and she's cool and precise. If the little lady, as you call her, wishes to risk her little lady's hide, that's fine with me. She'll be helping to save *my* hide."

"Now hold on! Who's giving the orders here?"

"I am, right now," Yates retorted. "This is something I personally know about, and you don't. Stop intruding your ignorance."

Sheriff Meek grumbled and sputtered, but grudgingly gave in. He eyed Jessie dubiously. "You sure you won't stay here?"

"Just long enough to change, Sheriff, not a minute more."

It didn't take long for her to switch into her own clothes, or for the sheriff to muster a posse from among the men in town. Voicing their support, they got the rigs on their horses in hot haste, and thundered out of town along the wagon trail heading southwest.

They set a fast pace, and while still a distance from the

154

first slope, Ki suddenly reined in and surveyed the terrain. Satisfied, he said, "We're turning northwest here."

Fifteen men and one woman turned horses and rode cross-country, with Ki leading the way, Jessie and the sheriff flanking him. The miles flowed steadily by, and their unflagging persistence paid off; shortly they reached a rugged rock barrier that brought hot memories back to Ki. He now veered them in a tight arc until they were riding directly toward the loom of the tall, massive hills, a fringe of thick forest along their common base like a green moat protecting gigantic, shattered battlements. They were perhaps two miles away when Ki eased them into a broad area of thickets and groves. At last he held up his hand as a signal to draw up. The posse clustered around while he dismounted and scouted the ground. Then he explained:

"The Red Devils, the half of them that are left, will either flee or head to their hideout. They're weakened and will likely move their hideout in case one of the prisoners talks, but they've no reason to quit. So they're going to be heading home, along here."

"Right along this path?" a posseman asked dubiously.

"Well, they can't move south and then west without being part mountain goat. They can avoid the spine of the Cascades by going west and then south, and if you'll look around you, you'll see the only logical way is through this section. There's reason for this path."

"Maybe they've already used it," another feared.

"No fresh prints," Ki responded. "If my hunch is right, and I wouldn't be here if I didn't think it was, all we've got to do is spread out on both sides and let them ride into us."

"If it's worth ridin' this far, boys, it's worth sittin' around for," Sheriff Meek added. "C'mon, let's get comfy."

The possemen seemed to know what was expected of

them, and they set about their tasks with swift, quiet efficiency. Rifles and ammunition were checked and distributed, and though Ki wasn't partial toward firearms, he accepted a Winchester .44-40 repeater in fair condition. Then they arranged themselves in a loose gantlet, hiding back far enough in the thickets alongside the trail to be shielded.

Lounging nervously in their saddles and smoking, the possemen waited, wishing somebody would come, but dreading what would happen. Sitting down, Ki lay the carbine crosswise on his knees and fixed his eyes on the crest of a rise a mile or so to the northeast. Jessie felt fatigued, and the wait stretched tiresomely, adding to her exhaustion. She soon found herself nodding, half dozing.

How long she had waited she couldn't tell, when abruptly Ki nudged her with his carbine and pointed toward the rise. A horseman was appearing above the crest, followed by another and another, riding at a leisurely pace, until Ki counted nine in all. They dipped nearer, often disappearing from view.

"It's your Devils," he told the others. "Steady now, wait till they're close. If they argue, hit hard with all you've got. They can sling lead, but we've got surprise on our side this time, for once."

Tensing ready, quivering with determination, the posse waited. The outlaws, riding in a leisurely fashion, were directly opposite the thicket when the posse crashed from the growth and Sheriff Meek's voice bellowed, "You're arrested! Elevate!"

There was a startled yelp, a volley of oaths. But the Red Devils did not obey the order, as with one accord they went for their guns.

Instantly the possemen surged into action along their gantlet. The long sweep of thundering guns swept in like an avenging tidal wave, and the outlaws, as vicious and callous a breed as any yet born, were caught in the middle. With yells of shock and pain, they turned to defend their exposed flanks, some digging in to fire a deadly response to the posse's challenge, while others dove off their horses for cover, desperate to reach the cover of the thickets, blasting back against the onslaught.

A few possemen charged both ends to prevent escapes along the path, but most turned the path and shouldering thickets into an inferno of pounding hoofs, rearing horses, roaring guns. Twice the Red Devils recoiled in wild pandemonium. Twice they managed to rally in a frantic effort to break out of this line of death. The attack became a close-quarters brawl of pistols and knives and hand-to-hand struggles with those caught within the path and thickets, while, with neither conscience nor mercy, volley after volley riddled those few outlaws who were able to flee.

Suddenly the shooting abated. The dust settled slowly, except where empty-saddled horses fishtailed skittishly. Possemen crowded around, whooping and laughing in victory, some converging on Ki to congratulate him on his hunch.

Ki smiled wanly, and wished it was as easy as that.

"Y'know," the sheriff remarked thoughtfully. "I've a notion we've just about bagged Red Duvall's gang. In all the time they've pestered me hereabouts, I never heard a report that made them out to be more'n twenty men. We got nine lyin' here an' yonder, and the railroaders got nine or ten, so there can't be more'n a couple still on the loose. Uh-huh, we've cleaned out a snake nest."

"Yes," Jessie agreed, "but the head of that snake is still free and living, and will grow a new body unless it's killed."

Sheriff Meek and the others nodded their agreement. But Everett Yates gazed at Jessie with the expression of a man

157

who was trying to pin down in his mind something vague and elusive.

An exultant posse started back to Forge. Trailing behind were nine led horses, each bearing the body of a dead Red Devil outlaw draped across its saddle.

Before they reached the wagon trail, the sheriff glanced over at Ki's roan, and saw that it was favoring its right rear leg.

"You're limping," he said.

"I am?" Dismounting, Ki checked his horse's fetlocks and hoofs, and nodded ruefully. "You're right. Looks like a bruise."

"How bad?" Jessie asked, coming alongside.

"Not much swelling. I think I'll walk him a bit."

"That'll take forever."

"All of you go on. I'll find a creek along here and plaster some mud on the leg."

"Okay, see you in town." The sheriff heeled his horse into motion again, the posse falling in behind with a few well-chosen tidbits of advice for Ki to ponder on his hike.

Ki stood by his roan until they had dropped from sight. Then carefully he pried the pebble out of its right rear shoe. The horse tested its hoof and took a few tender steps, but no damage had been done by Ki having wedged a pebble up underneath the shoe when none of the posse was looking.

Remounting, Ki rode toward an eastern stretch of hills, constantly watchful, cautious to pick terrain that would help conceal him. Once or twice the afternoon quiet was broken by freight trains steaming past, but otherwise the stillness was punctuated by normal small animal rustling and birds carrying on.

When he finally sighted Woody Fleishman's square, rugged house, Ki couldn't see anything particularly sinister or ghostly about it. It simply looked empty. Drawing near, he heard a dog howling—a long-drawn, mournful, persistent keening.

Ki quickened his horse's pace until he was in the shadow of the building. He swiftly dismounted, climbed the steps, and knocked on the thick front door. He waited, as before.

But nobody came, as before.

Ki knocked again, but only the dog's whining dirge answered. With some hesitation, Ki turned the knob and pushed the door. The door swung open a little, then seemed to catch. He pushed harder, and the door moved, yet still as though resisting his entrance, as though something was pressing against the other side.

Again he shoved, the opening widening. Through it leaped the wolf-dog, barking, nuzzling against him. "All right, Dog," Ki said, rubbing his head. "Let's see what's wrong."

Putting the dog aside, Ki pushed hard against the door and forced it open. Sunlight streamed in, and the first thing to catch his eye was a boot—a boot swinging pendulumlike, suspended not quite high enough to clear the opening door.

Ki stepped into the entry and stared upward, grimacing. The boot belonged to the stiffening man who hung swaying from a noose, the rope suspended from a stout staple driven into the beam above the door. The face staring back at Ki had glazed, bulging eyes and a purplish, swollen tongue. One side of the jaw was grotesquely swelled, the bald head twisted awry; all told, Jericho made an ugly corpse.

Glancing around, Ki saw a chair standing a little to one side of the door. He regarded it for a moment in relation to the hanging, and was moving it closer to stand on its seat, when suddenly the dog tensed, a low, ominous growling deep in his chest.

Swiftly Ki stepped forward and grabbed the dog's scruff. "What is it, Dog, is somebody outside? Easy now, we'll see."

The dog glared at the partially open door, teeth gleaming and growls welling. Tentative footfalls sounded outside on stone steps, then a voice called out, "Ki? Are you in there?"

"Jessie! Stay out, stay there!"

"Why should I stay . . ." Jessie began as she entered, then froze, stunned, Ki dragging a crazed dog back even as clashing fangs tore at her, and the foot of the hanging man almost brushed the top of her hair. Paling, she gasped, "Maybe I will, at that."

"No, better not move right now," Ki said, managing to calm the dog. "Good dog, you've done fine. She's a friend." The dog squatted on his haunches and cast a suspicious eye at Jessie. Ki smiled. "There. Now, what are you doing here?"

"Having a heart seizure," she replied weakly. "No, we need to talk. We might not get the chance, once we're back in town."

"I've a feeling it's coming to a boil, too." Ki stood on the chair to reach the dead man's face. It was cool, the flesh very firm. "But how'd you know where I'd be?"

"Oh, you'd feel a horse limping, Ki, so I knew it was a trick. But when I made my excuses and came back, you'd already gone a ways. I had to just follow you. Where are we, and who's that?"

"We're at Woody Fleishman's house, and this is Jericho." The swollen jaw interested Ki, and he passed sensitive fingertips along it as he talked to Jessie. "Jericho, I think, was a combination majordomo and guardian of a young woman who lived here, up to a few hours ago. He's not dead too long." Satisfied, Ki stepped down.

"Aren't you going to cut him down?"

"Let Sheriff Meek or a coroner do that. It'll be part of their investigation, and besides, taking him down will show that somebody was here after Jericho died."

"Well, we were here—*are* here. Why are you, Ki?"

"I wanted to find Fleishman," Ki answered, motioning the dog to come. "Now I'm afraid of what else we might find."

They made a thorough search of the house and stable, the dog trotting along beside Ki while keeping watch on Jessie. But there was no trace of Valerie or anyone else. And as they were checking the stable, and Ki was explaining some of what he'd seen and heard, Ki said there was something else missing:

"Manure, Jessie, other signs of horses. I got awakened by horses, footsteps, murmurings. And I know, by the way the stable's been used before, that it should have been used last night. But it wasn't. It's just the way it was when I came yesterday and left this morning."

Returning to the house, Jessie led the way upstairs and reentered what was undoubtedly Valerie's bedroom. "From what you say, Ki, what struck me as odd when we looked in the first time now makes a little more sense."

She began rifling through the drawers and wardrobe, and after a few minutes she nodded at Ki. "I thought as much. Look, her clothes are mussed, displaced, and not all here. I don't know what's been taken exactly, I just sense that there are gaps. She left, Ki, vamoosed."

For some moments he surveyed the disordered room, thinking intently. Then suddenly his eyes sparked and a thin half-smile quirked his lips.

Still smiling, Ki descended with Jessie and the dog to the entry, where the grisly presence over the door quickly stifled his good humor. He looked at the dog and pondered a moment, then took a chair and crashed the glass out of one window.

"Now it'll look like he got tired of staying here," he said to Jessie. "Let's get that door shut again and head for town."

161

"I agree. There's nothing more we can do here."

The dog whined as they strode to their horses, and mounting, Jessie said, "Don't get any ideas about keeping that beast, Ki."

He grinned. "No, but I'm going to try to deliver him."

They set off at a trot, the dog running after them.

★

Chapter 13

By the time Jessie and Ki arrived back in Forge, they'd thrashed out a number of puzzling aspects between them. Other details refused to clear up in a way that was satisfactory to Jessie, judging by her impatience as they stabled their horses.

"We really must find Woody Fleishman and Adams, if he's hit town," Jessie insisted. "And I should check for telegrams."

"Simple. You start at the depot and work up, and I'll start at the freightyard and work down. But I'd guess it's too quiet for Adams to be here, and Fleishman's a lost cause, long gone."

"It's hard to tell. We're here, though, so let's make sure."

Nodding agreement, Ki said, "I hope I'm wrong," and started up the main street with the dog trotting at his heels.

Jessie went to the depot, but the telegrapher didn't have any messages for her. Frustrated, she began hitting every shop and saloon along the street, which was livening up now, with the approach of evening. Early night-bloomers were cropping up among the plain folk doing business, the celebrating possemen and pals, and the railroad workers who'd quit or knocked off for the day. But no Rufus Adams, no Woody Fleishman, nor any word of them.

Ki has to be right, Jessie thought. *Adams isn't in town. When he comes, he'll be sowing a trail of powder, and I and everyone else will know he's here by the explosions in his wake.* And Fleishman was out of town—his freight clerk had told Ki he was, and indications were he'd not been home all day or night.

Yet right now this was her only straw, and Jessie was determined to grasp the hell out of it.

She entered Sneed's funeral parlor, where Adams would surely go. Bodies seemed to be stacked there like cordwood, some sheeted and some still dressed, mostly the victims of the attack at the cut, but interspersed with others, such as the nine slain by the posse.

The pudgy undertaker and Ted Baldwin were looking at the late Lou Quade, whom they'd evidently just laid out on the reception room davenport. As Jessie closed the door, Sneed glanced around. "We'll move him off in a jiffy, ma'am."

"I don't need to sit, thanks." She crossed and said to Baldwin, "Ki told me what happened." Then she leaned over Quade.

"Yeah, I was there, almost. 'Nough for the sheriff to make me help carry Quade over here. Hey, Ki was looking at that, too."

"Madam!" Sneed gasped. "If you please!"

Ignoring them, Jessie had opened the corpse's shirt and was examining the knife sheath at his waist. "Remember the

164

knife that was tossed at Isabelle and me yesterday, Ted? It was a skinner's, and it'd just about be a perfect fit to slip into this."

"And into lots of other sheaths, too," Baldwin stated defensively. "Why d'you hafta pick on Quade, one of my men?"

"Because he tried to kill Ki. Ted, I'll explain more fully when there's time and more proof. First, tell me, you've got that property agreement your father made with Adams, haven't you?"

"How'd you know about that?" Baldwin asked, startled.

"Never mind how. You've kept it safe, haven't you?"

"Why, ah, it's safe, I reckon, it's just not with me," Baldwin faltered. "It went to square me at the Nugget."

"To pay gambling debts?" Jessie frowned in bewilderment. "It doesn't add— Ted, you really sold it to George Chaber?"

"George refused it. Woody Fleishman bought it for cash."

"Ah, now that fits," Jessie said happily.

"What in tunket are you talking about?" Baldwin demanded.

Jessie didn't have the chance to explain, even if she'd cared to, for at that moment a rickety wobble-wheel wagon and a lathered, steaming team pulled up in front of the parlor. The noise was horrendous, Rufus Adams bellowing at the team to whoa up, at passersby in his way, and at Sneed as he clomped in on his splinted leg.

"Sneed! Sneed, you got Gene Trevarro here?"

"In our rear quarters," the fat undertaker intoned apprehensively. "We're holding him according to sheriff's orders."

"Well, you ain't holdin' Gene no more!" Adams's ferocious eyes swept the reception room, but he dismissed everybody and everything he saw as unimportant, and roared at Sneed, "Show me the body so's I can identify it. If it is my half-brother, I'll skin some filthy rascal alive! I'll tear this cussed town apart!"

Sneed scurried toward the back, Adams barging after and almost stepping on him. Jessie and Baldwin exchanged glances, and moved quickly to the rear quarters, just in time to hear Adams let loose a blistering cry and whack his cane on something harder than Sneed. Sneed could be heard saying, "There, there."

"Get your filchfingers off'n me! Just put Gene in the best coffin you got, an' gussy him up for a first-class funeral tomorrow."

The front door banged open just then, and Sheriff Meek came trotting into the parlor. "Where is that troublemaker?"

"I'm in the back, but I'm comin' out!" Adams hollered, and thrusting Sneed aside, he stormed bumpingly out to confront the sheriff. "You're invited to the burial—each an' every one of 'em."

"I'm handling this case, Rufus. You ain't above the law."

"Depends on how small the law is to begin with," Adams snapped, and then seemed to notice Baldwin for the first time. "No, I don't peg you for shotgunnin' Gene instead o' me," he said loudly, slightly contemptuously. "You know me too well to make that error."

"Damn right," Baldwin shot back, flushing red from his neck up. "And I ain't apologizin' to you for nothin'."

"You've made your drunk boastin'," Adams snorted. "When I got time, I'll see you get the chance to live up to it."

"Come smokin' when you're ready. Personally, I've had a change o' mind about you, and wouldn't harm one flea on your white-haired, hollow head—lest, of course, you shoot first."

166

Adams moved to go. "There's some comin' up now."

"There's been too much already," Jessie declared, and the sheriff stubbornly got in Adams's way, saying, "Hold on, she's right. You ain't popular in Forge, and you'd better not stir up any more trouble than there is already. I'm warning you."

"You've warned me," Adams snarled, brushing the sheriff aside and hobbling forward. "Now stay outta my way!"

Sheriff Meek stood for a moment, cranking his mustache. "Gawd, I guess I just have to keep after. Comin', Miss Starbuck?"

"I would, but I'm looking for Woody Fleishman."

Baldwin glanced at her. "About anything I can help with?"

Jessie just shook her head and walked toward the door. Ted could be likeable and earnest enough, and she gave the young rooster credit for standing up to Adams. Change of mind, indeed! Change of heart was more like it, whether Isabelle realized it or not. Who could tell, Isabelle might straighten out this feud better than anything. A man can't go on fighting his wife's relations, and grandfathers have a way of having their notions changed for them. In the meantime, Jessie wondered how Ki was faring.

He had gone up the street, strongly hoping not to meet Woody Fleishman while he still had Valerie's dog. So, instead of going all the way to the freightyard, Ki turned the far corner of the druggist's into the alley, mounted the outside stairs, and knocked on Martha's door. Just as before, it took persistence.

Footsteps, finally, and Martha's voice: "Go away!"

"It's Ki. Let me in."

"I'm busy. I said I'd be here, not that I'd be alone."

"I know who you're with," Ki said, which wasn't wholly true, and could prove embarrassing if he was wrong. "Now, we can talk about them real loud through the door, or you can trust me and open."

"Bastard," she said, and unlocked the door a crack.

The dog plowed past Martha, who stumbled back with door in hand. Ki stepped in, nodded pleasantly to Martha, then greeted the couple who sat at the room's big table.

"Good afternoon, George, Valerie. I thought you might miss your dog, Valerie, so I brought him to you. He missed you."

The dog was resting his head on Valerie's knee, and she looked pleased but definitely startled. George Chaber only smiled his thin, mocking smile and nodded cordially to Ki, saying, "Thanks, Ki. I like knowing early when I've failed."

"Have you? I got here by coincidence. Being in the right place at the right time, and making a wild stab in the dark. Oh, trying to pin the blame on me failed. I wasn't even a suspect. When I got up, Jericho was already out tracking with the dog. Still, it wasn't a bad twist for a spur-of-the-moment plan."

"Sorry," Valerie said. "I didn't know what else to do."

"True, Ki, it wasn't a good night to spend the night."

"I think it was. A good night for a ride, too."

Chaber smiled, and did not pursue the subject. Martha, having shut the door, was tugging smooth her Mother Hubbard and giving Ki more suspiciously quizzical glances.

Valerie asked, "But how did you get Dog away from the house? I wouldn't have thought Jericho would let him go."

In a few terse sentences, Ki related what he and Jessie had found at the house. George Chaber swore under his breath. Valerie turned white at the lips, her large eyes beginning to swim.

"I suppose Jericho did it because I . . . I escaped him," she quavered. "I've wanted out almost since I moved in, eight months ago. Woody was kind, but the horrid men working for him always came drinking and gambling at all hours. I got frightened to death of them, but Woody set Jericho to guard me, to stop me from going out."

"To stop you from feeling, too. All you felt was terror."

"Yes, Ki, then George came. First I feared him, like I feared you, but when I *felt*...! Well, the difference with George is, he's getting me to feel more and more, continuously. We made plans, and when I learned Woody wasn't to be back till today, I tricked Jericho last night with some knockout drops George gave me."

"And George drove you here in a big buggy," Ki finished, turning to Martha, "to stay with an old friend from . . . ?"

"From some old days, leave it at that," Martha said, a bit of crispness in her tone. "How about some coffee, or cake?"

"No thanks, I have to be going," Ki said. "One thing, George. How come Fleishman allowed you to visit Valerie?"

Chaber shrugged, though the mocking gleam in his eyes seemed more pronounced. "Woody wanted me to invest cash in his freight business. When I went out the first time, out of courtesy, I met Valerie. After that I strung him along with money, not for his investment, but to have excuses to visit. He couldn't very well refuse."

"Men can be stupid where women are concerned," Valerie added. "I pretended to despise George, and Woody never tumbled."

"*I* tumbled," Chaber admitted. "She got to me."

"You got to yourself," Ki said. "For you to get her to feel, you had to do it first, George, and look at you now. You've got the look of a cat that's just swiped a saucer of cream and sees the door of the canary cage open." He chuckled, then turned grave. "I know you're planning to, anyway, but keep out of sight—the dog too. There may be more to this than a jealous, angry man."

Chaber frowned slightly, but nodded. "I've an idea you've got good reasons for thinking that."

"I have." Ki patted the dog's head, smiled at the couple, and whispered in Martha's ear as he left the room.

Returning to the street, Ki immediately went to the freightyard and learned from the clerk that, sorry, Mr. Fleishman had left for the day two to three hours ago. So Ki moved on down the street, stopping at each place and not surprised to hear that, sorry, Mr. Fleishman hadn't been seen today. After all, three hours ago was about when the posse arrived back in town. Figure a half hour for the word to spread, and Fleishman's departure made sense, as well as his leaving town for much longer than a day.

Shortly, Ki had worked his way down past the druggist's. He was coming out of a bootmaker's shop when he glimpsed a runaway wagon team on the other side of the Black Nugget, tearing up the street toward it as though to crash through its doors. Then he realized it wasn't a runaway, but an insane driver hurtling along lickety-split, with no thought of his or anyone else's safety.

The wagon and brace reared to a halt, spewing gravel and dusty grit in a great cloud. The driver tossed his reins to a roustabout idling near the hotel door, then clambered down and lurched toward the entrance. Ki didn't have to be close to recognize the grizzled visage of Rufus Adams, but he couldn't be sure why the old man was so ungainly—it seemed he had a large stovepipe section strapped to his right leg, but that couldn't be.

Ki checked a few more joints, and came out of the last one to find Hilliard Latwick standing in the bed of Adams's wagon. Too far away to hear, Ki had a sick feeling that those gathering around were listening to more hate fever, the hotel owner gesturing expansively and puffing and

170

spouting like a walrus. Latwick had surfaced damn quickly, too, for Ki had spent maybe one to two minutes per spot, or three if he needed to ask a bartender. Latwick must have been wound up and ready to spew the instant Adams charged in for his kinfolk.

A couple more stores, then Ki entered a small mercantile. Jessie caught up with him in there, and led him out to the recessed doorway, where Nanette Thrall and Sheriff Meek were waiting. They both looked concerned, but Nanette was more distressed, while the sheriff was ponderously grim, as if flummoxed as well as worried.

Nanette asked, "Have you found George?"

"I've been hunting Fleishman," Ki hedged, and eyed Jessie sharply. "Why? Have we been looking for the wrong man?"

Jessie shook her head. "No. Nanette knows where he is."

"Fleishman? Here in town?"

"In the Black Nugget, Ki, where my girls and I have our rooms." Nanette's eyes were alive with anxiety as she explained. "A couple of hours ago, Latwick told me our strict 'no gentlemen' rule was going to be waived awhile for Woody Fleishman. I objected, but I work for George, and Latwick's like a partner. Next thing I know, gunmen are lounging near my wing's door. Then, a few minutes ago, Rufus Adams blows in, and not Latwick, but Fleishman comes offering to take Adams back to see how the Trevarros are fine and so forth. Now I've got two men back there where men have no business!"

"Nanette came to me, and I...well, those gunslicks wouldn't budge or let me by, or do nothin' I told them." The sheriff's face flushed, his jaw hardened from the humiliation, for Meek was no coward. "They dared me to draw, and I...didn't."

"You acted right," Jessie declared. "You've got a ticklish situation, with the potential of that whole bunch of girls as hostages."

"Thanks, Miss Starbuck, but I do hate to crawfish. Anyway, when we ran into you, and knowed you folks was so het up to find Fleishman, I thought maybe you knew something that'd help."

"I have a good idea what's going on there," Jessie replied. "Fleishman has Adams cornered with the Trevarros, and he's likely rushing through the deal he's been aiming at ever since Adams filed on the mineral rights of Moon Trail Canyon."

"Fleishman? I can't believe it!"

"You'd be believing it like gospel, if Fleishman's orders hadn't been bungled and the wrong man killed the night before last."

"If that's so, why hasn't Fleishman tried to kill Adams again?"

"He's likely aiming to, but the setup is different now. Adams has relatives who'll inherit if he dies. Fleishman didn't know this before, but now he does."

"And we're wasting time. Nanette, is there a back way?"

"Why, yes, Ki. A regular back door. No key. Locked, of course, against two-legged animals, but the key's been lost for centuries." She paused, brightening. "I have a key, a master room key, that I was once told might fit that lock. I don't know."

"Wonderful," Jessie said. "Can you get it quickly?"

"Gentlemen, turn your backs."

Sheriff Meek and Ki dutifully turned around. The sheriff muttered a bit, then said, "I gotta warn you both that this is plumb dangerous. I'll try to protect you, but I can't guarantee it."

"There, gentlemen. And, Sheriff, if you all aren't safe,

then what they claim is true." Nanette handed the key to Jessie.

"Just show me proof!" Meek exclaimed. "Or is that a waste of time too?"

"Sheriff, say we're wrong. You still want in, don't you?"

"Ki," the sheriff demanded querulously, "do you always get the best of folks?" He rushed on, not expecting a reply. "Raise your right hands. Fine. You're now duly sworn deputy sheriffs."

"Well, I'd like to stand on my hind feet and put in my bit," Nanette said resentfully, but Jessie took her aside and explained that she needed Nanette to tell Yates what was going on.

While Nanette hustled down toward the trainyard, the other three made their way along the first side alley they came to, and entered the darkened rear field that ran behind most of the nearby buildings. From there they turned toward the hotel, sprinting along the hilly, trash-heaped ground to the corner of the building across from the Black Nugget. They drew in and listened, scanning the area. Beneath the long rear overhang, either half of the Black Nugget had its own deeply recessed rear entry, thus making the hotel one about a quarter of the way along the rear length.

Jessie whispered, "Listen, Nanette told me a few details. From the rear door, there's a hall that goes to the wing's lobby door. About eight, ten feet inside is a stairwell to the upper rooms. She doesn't know where Fleishman is, but the Trevarros are up in room 227, next to hers, just a couple from the stairs."

"That all?" the sheriff groaned mournfully. "We oughta just go in there and shoot ourselves and get it over with. They're already howling for our blood, I can hear 'em."

"For Rufus Adams's neck, "Ki said, indicating the street. "Latwick's out there stirring a hornets' nest with a short stick. It may be a question of who gets to Adams first. Let's rush—"

"Wait! Let's get up on that overhang like Quade did."

"Sheriff, Quade never climbed up. No ladders. My window was opened to make it seem that they'd scaled up, so that Latwick wouldn't be nailed for giving them a key."

"Why would Latwick do that? What's his stake in the game?"

"Woody Fleishman couldn't do it alone," Jessie answered. "Now, are we ready? Careful, that back door is probably guarded."

"What for? Nobody can open it," said the sheriff, hustling as swiftly and quietly as he ever had. All three darted fleetingly on their toes as much as possible, their backs flat against the rear wall of the building, Jessie gripping her custom .38, the sheriff hefting a warhorse of a Remington .44 in his fist.

They were mere yards away, able to see some of the deep recess of the doorway. The sheriff's boot toe clicked against a tin can. Instantly there was a startled movement in the doorway.

"Whozzat?" called a man. "Speak up or I fire!"

"You're arrested!" Sheriff Meeks yelled, and launched forward in a bandy-legged charge. Ki sprang after, trying to race faster and edge around forward to catch the man in a crossfire.

Orange flame lanced out of the man's pistol once, then again. In the light of the muzzle flashes, the guard in standard working clothes and the onrushing sheriff were outlined. Then the man, having located the sheriff, leveled his gun for a point-blank shot.

Ki sprang into a *tobi-geri*, a flying snap-kick, aiming to strike the man's solar plexus. Simultaneously with his spring, the man shifted targets and pulled the trigger, his pistol

174

discharging a bullet that snapped by Ki's ear. And Sheriff Meek desperately shot the man in the chest. The man lurched from the slug's impact, and Ki slammed into him off-center, clipping his ribs. The man reeled sideways against the recessed supports, slack-jawed, falling in a spiraling crumple as his legs gave beneath him. He landed faceup, the final pumpings of his heart spreading crimson across his chest.

"What idjit trick was that, bouncin' at him unarmed an' all?" the sheriff cried at Ki. "I came nigh to pluggin' you instead!" Then he looked down at the body. "Jake Ulrich!"

Ki, who was kneeling beside Ulrich, ripped open his shirt. He grinned in satisfaction as he revealed something strapped around the dead man's waist—a lizardskin moneybelt.

"Eugene Trevarro's, I bet you'll find," he said, handing it up. "Proof enough that Ulrich was one killer, and fits in well with his partner Quade's tries on Jessie and me."

"You never did tell me why you're bein' attacked—but, hell, this ain't the time or place! Let's get goin' with that key!"

Moving to the rear door, Jessie hunkered down, took out the key, and slid it in. Carefully she turned the key, to find it stuck either from age or lack of fit. She strained against it. It moved, grinding ages of rust between its teeth. Then, finally, the latch clunked all the way back, and she pushed the door ajar.

Something warm and wet dripped on her hand. She glanced up and saw the sheriff hunching over her, swaying slightly, his left elbow crooked as if his arm were a broken wing. "Sheriff! You've been hit!"

"Only a flesh wound," he said firmly. "C'mon!"

He strode forward, his revolver leveled in his right hand, blood running down his left arm and dripping from his fingertips.

Ki now realized why they still had some edge of surprise left. For one thing, the corridor reverberated with noise, seeming to magnify the sounds and blend them into incoherence. Second, the noises were coming from the front of the hotel — a crescendo of galloping hooves, angry shouting men, and scattered pistol fire — so that anyone who normally would have been back here, or watching here, was busy viewing the excitement out in the street. They came very close to the stairwell before they were discovered.

One of six men guarding the area happened to glance up and spot them. "Gawddamn!" he blurted, and began firing feverishly.

Within seconds the confining corridor was filled with the blasting of revolvers and the acrid odor of blinding powdersmoke. Two fell before the accurate fire of Jessie and the sheriff. Ki, springing high and racing as fast as he could to maintain his arcing momentum, crossed the lead-flinging no-man's-land in the middle of the hall by practically running along the wall. Then, lashing out with a leaping kick, he dropped to the flooring, the man he'd kicked clutching his hemorrhaging belly.

Now at the stairwell, Ki pivoted and rammed the heel of his palm to another gunman's temple, fracturing the man's skull. Jessie blasted a hole through the chest of a man targeting Ki in his pistol sights. And Ki, glimpsing another gunman scrambling up the stairs to spread a warning, lunged after him. The man suddenly felt Ki jump on his back, and his legs go out from under him so that he fell against the treads. Then he felt excruciating pain, and after that nothing, as Ki grabbed both of his ankles and pulled violently up and backward. A scream, a dull cracking noise, and the man died, his back broken and spinal cord severed. Ki rolled him off the stairs, where he fell on the head of another gunman, sending them both crashing to the stairwell floor.

176

"Guard the stairs!" he yelled at the wounded sheriff, but Meek only laughed derisively and plunged up the stairs with Jessie, taking the risk of leaving enemies on their backtrail.

"There it is!" Sheriff Meek shouted, diving by Ki, spraying blood like a dog shagging its coat after a soaking.

He's committing suicide, Jessie thought. *Isn't there any way to stop it?*

None. No respite to sit down and talk this over. But if Sheriff Meek went out, he'd be going out in the style of his choosing, showing these gunslicks that the law was not to be ignored or derided or made to crawfish.

She was a step behind Ki as the sheriff, using his good right shoulder, hurled himself against room 227's hall door. The barrier had been cheap to begin with, and was made flimsier by lack of upkeep. It splintered inward without effort. Sheriff Meek, bloody and furious, stumbled across the threshold amid the wreckage of the door. A tall, lean, bronzed man leaped over his body and landed in the room in a fighting crouch.

Facing them were Woody Fleishman and three muscle-bound lads with short-barreled brushguns. Adams was at Fleishman's side, and both were leaning over a table on which were legal documents, a pen, and a heavy buckskin pouch. Over against one wall, Consuela Trevarro stood with her arms around Isabelle.

A split instant of reaction time, a heartbeat of perceiving and evaluating before acting . . . and in that moment, Jessie strode in through the door and yelled, "Rufus, he killed Gene! Fleishman killed your brother!"

Woody Fleishman whirled about, his hands darting for a pair of .44 pistols. The three men with brushguns threw them up, Fleishman shouting to them, "Gun 'em! Gun 'em all!"

All hell broke loose in the small room. A large chunk

of ceiling and a piece of the wall by the door were torn away as the murderous short-barrels belched fire and wide-patterned shot. But Jessie had fired first, blasting the nearest shotgunner just as he was in the process of squeezing the trigger. And Ki sent a *shuriken* speeding toward a second man, while diving the short distance and using a forward snapkick followed by a sideways elbow-smash to cave in the third man's ribs. The *shuriken* sliced into the second man's throat in unison with Sheriff Meek's final shot, the sheriff now sitting on the floor against the wall.

Rufus Adams was like a man possessed. He finally had something to get his teeth into—and he did, biting Woody Fleishman on the wrist before the man could level his gun on him or any of the women. He grappled to obtain the other pistol, releasing the chewed wrist to roar, "Assign over my mineral rights, huh? As if that isn't what you're after, you said!"

But Fleishman was every bit as wily and tough as he was reputed to be. He raised one pistol in a lightning move and brought its barrel down on old Adams's head in a vicious blow. Rufus Adams shuddered and, still clawing blindly at Fleishman, crashed to his hands and knees.

Two women screamed shrilly in terror—while the third, Jessie, dodged out of the powdersmoke to snap a shot at Fleishman. But Adams got in her way. Scrambling woozily from the floor, the old lumberman lunged across the room at Fleishman like a maniac, all the while hollering at Fleishman some of what Fleishman must have taunted him with: "Gonna throw us to the mob, were you? Me an' my two kinswomen would have our necks stretched unless I signed the quitclaim, eh?"

Ki was forced to hold back his attack as Adams blundered diagonally in front of him. Leaping backward out of the bulling Adams's way, Fleishman managed to get in one shot, staggering the old man but failing to stop him. Alarmed, Fleishman stepped back again, and his leg struck against the windowsill just as Adams reached him. Off-balance, Fleishman started falling out the window.

"Oh, no you don't!" bellowed Adams, reaching out and down. He got Fleishman around the throat and hauled him bodily through the window. "You low-livered, sneaking cockroach!" Adams ranted, holding him up virtually nose to nose and shaking him as a dog would a rat. "I'll strip your mangy carcass and nail it to my . . . my . . ."

He slowed then to a stop, and released the limp-necked, twisted ragdoll in his hands. Fleishman collapsed, looking rather more like Jericho in death than he had in life, Ki thought.

Adams stood there for a moment, staring stupidly down at Fleishman. Then he turned around and made an apologetic gesture toward his two kinswomen, took a wobbly step toward Sheriff Meek, and sat down hard beside him. Blood was welling around the black hole in his shirt now. He didn't bother looking at it, but smiled at the sheriff and said, "How're you doin', Oswald?"

And Meek, nodding weakly, grinned back. "Just fine, Rufus, how about yourself?"

Chapter 14

The room filled, then swelled with people.

Through the smashed door came a strange procession of townsfolk—railroaders, dance-hall girls, boozers. A blacksmith came carrying his hammer, and an old lady arrived in a contraption of a wheelchair, and there was a defrocked priest around for a while, asking when the sandwiches were to be served.

But among the first, luckily, came Doc Elgin, Sneed, Everett Yates, Ted Baldwin, and the Pace boys. The twins were dragging a frightened and torn Hilliard Latwick between them, who slithered in on his knees, pleading for his life.

The room was already crowded with women. Consuela Trevarro squatted next to Adams, stanching his wound with strips of his shirt. Her daughter, Isabelle, was laughing and crying hysterically in Ted Baldwin's arms. Nanette waltzed in, got into the spirit, and started to cry, flinging herself down by Sheriff Meek and anxiously exploring to see how badly the astonished lawman was hit. Doc Elgin worked as best he could under the circumstances.

"Collected some crew and larruped for town," Ian Pace explained to Ki. "This pig-bladder was in the boss's wagon, a-whompin' up a necktie party. You must've heard us breaking it up."

"With my help," Everett Yates added, sliding an exploratory arm around Jessie. "Thank God you're safe, that you both are."

"I wouldn't have been, if there'd been one more woman," Ki declared. "Too much weeping, wailing, and nursing for me."

"Well, don't go yet," Jessie asked. "In fact, I could use a hand gathering some of the people around the sheriff and Adams."

Soon a small group of those most involved was formed. Once Doc Elgin pronounced both wounded men out of danger, Jessie spoke.

"This won't take long, no need to, you can fit all the pieces together yourselves. But there are a few details that it might be nice to share. Such as yours, Rufus, that the three men who killed your half-brother have died. And you, Ted, if you don't mind my advice."

"He'll take and like it," Isabelle answered for him.

"Ted, Fleishman extracted the agreement to help him pull a crime. That's illegal, so you get it back. But face it, you don't want the canyon, even if you could pay, and when you may get it through family ties anyway. The best thing would be to take the agreement and destroy it."

"Yeah, before it causes us any more grief." Baldwin went to the table and began riffling through papers. "Whoa up! These are all made out to a Latham Daws, not Woodrow Fleishman."

Ki chuckled. "Same man, different name. He felt it growing too hot here for Fleishman, so he was preparing to scram as Daws."

"Oh, I see." Baldwin located his agreement and tore it up.

"Now, Rufus, you're free to sell Everett here the right-of-way. And, Everett, since you know Rufus is trying to help out the Trevarros, you might be a little more generous in your terms."

"My word," Yates vowed. "Rufus, I'll meet you half-way."

"I reckon I was a mite touchy at judgin' railroads," Adams allowed gruffly. "And young Ted, I misjudged you, too."

"Well, it cuts both ways," Ted replied solemnly. "Was I a fool, and was I took by Fleishman?" He blinked and said, "But wait a minute. Who *was* Fleishman?"

While the others were murmuring conjectures and denials, Jessie went across to the body, knelt, and brushed back the thick mat of neckline beard. "No doubt. It's Red Duvall."

"When you identified him as Red Duvall, you took everyone's breath away," Everett Yates began, rubbing soap into a lather on his hairy chest. "I remember you saying his nickname came from a hang-rope scar, not red hair. And Ki saying that once this fact was known, it narrowed the suspects down to full-bearded men."

"Or priests with high collars," Jessie added, marching naked into the bathroom. "Or Arab chieftains with turbans."

"What I want to know is how you and Ki got suspicious of Fleishman in the first place, to even consider checking his beard."

"A very little slip," Jessie answered, climbing into the tall broad porcelain tub with Yates. "He didn't know Border Mex."

182

"You mean Spanish?"

"No, I mean Mexican Spanish that's garbled even worse all along the border. It helps to know Castilian Spanish, but no guarantee. Well, I was with Fleishman in the Black Nugget when Isabelle came up, and I asked her in a simple five-word sentence to show off her clothes. Everett, a boy of eight knows that much, but Fleishman—Duvall—thought she wanted to dance with him, after I planted that notion in his head. So I knew that whoever he was, he wasn't from Calexico, and that was the first tipoff."

She took the soap away from him, saying, "Here, let me do that." She ran the soap gently down his back and sides, and conveniently forgot to tell Everett of her telegram to the ranch, requesting information on Fleishman or a man of his description. The lateness of a reply indicated that the researchers were having trouble getting information—which they should, if the man had never been in that area. Now, as Jessie lathered with hands gentle, almost caressing, down along his buttocks, Everett squirmed a little but swore he was listening to her talking.

"Well, Duvall sensed that he'd stumbled, that I'd caught out his Fleishman character and would eventually expose it. So I had to die. The attempts before were serious, true, but aimed at any Starbuck intruder on general principles. I was a personal threat, and when Ki stayed overnight at Fleishman's house, Duvall must have felt extremely keen on killing us. He came close, but he failed. Like most criminals, Duvall's error was a tiny detail."

"You're right, Jessie. Like packing an odd-caliber gun, or being the only man handling messages that end up compromised."

"Turn around," she directed, then said, "What do you mean?"

"The Red Devils knew too darn much about what was going on in my railroad. That meant somebody on the inside was passing information." Yates gasped a little, although Jessie was sure her hands were being very gentle. "When you sent word that you and Ki were coming, I knew I didn't babble it, and I knew only two could have—the telegrapher or Virgil. I set a small trap, I didn't even tell you, and Virgil sprung it."

"I'm sorry to hear it. What . . . ?"

"He didn't walk out of it," Yates said, then changed the subject by asking, "What are your plans for tomorrow morning?"

"Bright and early, I'm afraid. I still haven't visited my Snowshoe Mines, and I need to interview a miner named Cervant as possible manager. He comes recommended by Baldwin and Adams."

"Good, the timing's right for me staying the night in *your* accommodations for a change." He reached out and put soap froth on her nipples. "Would Fleishman have bought the mine?"

"No, that was simply a gambit, a test to see what I knew. Rather common, that sort. What was unusual about Duvall were his brains and imagination." Jessie refrained from adding that the cartel had spotted these qualities and hired him, and she also made sure that her talk about Duvall made him sound like an individual, not an internationally controlled force.

Yates said, "No doubt Duvall knew the railroads threatened his survival. But he couldn't stop, only slow our progress."

"Oh, Duvall wasn't kidding himself. He wanted to control the railroad because he knew it was unstoppable and would eventually be profitable. So he put all his money into stocks—not railroad stocks, which would look funny for a freightwagon owner to hold—but the next best thing, the bank, where everybody except him held shares in the railroad. He was the largest bank shareholder, and when he busted you bad enough, Everett, he'd have gone to his pals at the bank and told them he could do your job, if given authority."

Yates said dreamily, "I think I'd have given it to him."

He was crouching, putting his hands under Jessie's thighs and lifting her. She lifted easily. She rose up and then sank down, fitting herself around him.

"Ohh," he breathed.

"Yes . . ." she answered, eyes closed . . .

"But, Ki, how did you figure out that the Red Devils attacking the construction project would come through by you, instead of heading straight for the hills?"

"Because," Ki said, and opened another button on Martha's blouse. They were in the alcove bed again, and Ki was pleased to be unwrapping something besides that Mother Hubbard. "Because I figured they'd been badly mauled and lost half their ranks, and they'd head for Fleishman's house. The house was their logical hideout, where they cached their loot. The home of respectable Mr. Fleishman, where nobody would dare dream of heading."

Ki began working on another button. Martha laughed a little and opened all the rest of them herself. Ki pushed her blouse back so that one of her breasts thrust out, and he said,

"By being respectable, Fleishman was able to find out things. He knew that big money was in the bank on payday. He learned that from Wilkes, who thought he was all right." Ki jiggled her bared breast in his hand, and she stared down at it as though she had never really looked at it before. "That's why I told Sheriff Meek that when he goes out to cut down old Jericho, he'll probably find a lot of the holdup money looted from the payday robbery."

Martha jumped when Ki put his lips and then his whole mouth around one of her nipples. She acted as though she expected Ki to bite it, but in a minute she was stroking his hair and pressing his head to her. Her voice was a little breathless when she asked, "Why did Jericho hang himself?"

Ki released her nipple to answer, "He didn't, Martha. Duvall hung him, or rather hung his body to make it look as if Jericho had done himself in. When Duvall came home and found that Jericho had let Valerie escape, he evidently got so mad that he beat the man to death. When I examined Jericho, I found that his jaw had been broken, and his neck too, but not by the rope. The break was too high up for that. The rope was around Jericho's neck, all right, but his neck was hardly swollen at all. It would have been, if he'd died by hanging."

He sighed and said, "Anyway, it's all over now, and I'd just as soon change the subject. It's pretty morbid, talking about men being hung."

A wicked smile pulled at Martha's lips as she reached down and grasped the conspicuous bulge in Ki's trousers. "I agree," she said. "But I guess some men *get* hung, and others are just that way naturally..."